Fundamentals of Chinese Medicine

MEDICAL PULSE DIAGNOSIS® (MPD®)

ROBERT DOANE, L.Ac.
MARCUS GADAU, Ph.D.

Fundamentals of Chinese Medicine Medical Pulse Diagnosis (MPD®)
Second edition, published 2019

Author Robert K. Doane
Pulse Illustrations by Stephanie Parcus
Copyright ©2019, Lucky Falcon LLC, All rights reserved

SOFT COVER ISBN: 978-1-942661-35-1
HARD COVER ISBN: 978-0-989455-17-6

Published by Lucky Falcon, LLC in cooperation with Kitsap Publishing

For more information about the author and MPD®, visit www.doane.us
For more information about publishing, visit www.KitsapPublishing.com

Contents

Brilliant Book for Beginners in pulse diagnosis

"This book is one of the best I have read for beginners in the art of pulse diagnosis. Having said that there is lots of new information as well for those who are experienced. There are many good features to this book but one that I liked was the treatment strategy for pathological pulses. Rather than detailing which Herb or acupoint or combinations to use this strategy talked in general principles or strategies. For example, if the pulse reveals a Blood Stasis with Qi and Blood Deficiency then the treatment strategy is to invigorate blood 70-80% plus tonify and nourish blood -20-30 %. This gives the reader or practitioner a lot of options to employ whether acupuncture/ herbs/ nutrition etc. Such information can be applied using other therapies including Western Herbal Medicine/Naturopathy. In fact, although this book is primarily aimed for the Chinese Medicine market it could easily be used by other practitioners such as Medical Doctors, physiotherapists, etc. Once the guiding principles are arrived at then there are endless treatment possibilities. In summary, a must-read for all Therapists!!"

~ Peter Farnsworth

MPD has revolutionized my practice

"An essential book for anyone wanting to master pulse diagnosis! This systematic approach is clear and easy to follow. MPD has revolutionized my practice. 100% more practical and applicable to real-world Clinical practice than what was taught in school. I especially like this as a Clinic handbook reference guide with percentages of treatment principles for each aberrant pulse. Shows details on pulse positions so as not to get confused.

Although this is not a book with herbal recommendations, Bob is extremely generous with herbal details and suggestions on Doane.us and the DNA/MPD Facebook page. After you get this book, practice it and get hands-on training for confirmation! A true revolution for our medicine."

~ John F

Written by practitioners for practitioners. Love it.

"This is a good quality paperback book with great legibility. The graphics are great and all are supported by the text. You don't have to flip through pages to find which graphic is being referred to! It's obvious a lot of thought went into the end users experience. It is intelligently written & practically applicable. I use this method on a daily basis in my practice. It is the first time I feel I have gotten a good understanding of pulse diagnosis that makes sense in both TCM & Western Medicine."

~ Sinead Dee

Clear and Concise

"This style of pulse diagnosis makes so much sense! After reading the book you can instantly apply the pulse taking skill to your clinic. The illustrations and descriptions are clear and concise. The book is simple, but you may need to read it over a few times and keep practicing on every person you meet.

I have been using this method of pulse diagnosis for the past year. It's been really helpful in the clinic. I have been to both Jimmy Chang's and Bob Doane's workshops, and absolutely recommend learning directly from them."

~ **Michael**

A MUST for the clinician!

"Finally a concise manual on how to effectively take the pulse. These are the most crucial skills of any acupuncturist and this manual makes it easy to study, practice and utilize the Chinese medical pulse system in your clinic. Can't wait for a follow-up edition that includes herbs to treat these pulse presentations!"

~ **KL**

Watching and Learning is Believing

"Watching Bob's team perform so much and being so accurate is enough to make anyone a believer. Through years of learning from many different sources, bob has perfected his DNA method to be one of the best. Bob teaches his method all over the world and domestically to many students eager to learn. The accuracy I have seen over the years is amazing not only to me but to all who witness it. Then being able to diagnose a treatment program that produces the best results. Thank you, Bob, for all you have done and continue to do for the industry."

~ **Tom Taylor,** Professional Marketing

Learn pulse diagnosis on another level, highly recommend

"Clear and concise, yet thorough. A great reference for learning an effective pulse diagnosis system delivered in a digestible format! Highly recommended."

~ **Anonymous**

Acknowledgments

Acknowledgment of Dr. Zhang Wei Yan (Jimmy Chang), O.M.D.
First and foremost, I must give thanks to my greatest teacher of pulse diagnosis, Dr. Zhang Wei Yan. His unique insight and impassioned instruction of this medicine gave me the necessary tools to practice Chinese Medicine to its full potential. While my discoveries and perspective on pulse diagnosis have become uniquely my own over the past twenty years, much of the material in the pages that follow is a variation on his approach. His teaching has inspired a generation of practitioners to learn Chinese pulse diagnosis and thereby significantly improving patient care.

Thanks to Dr. Hubert Heinrichs, M.D.
Many thanks to Dr. Heinrichs for his contribution. He is a seasoned physician and an expert in the MPD method. His editing and input were invaluable in creating the current book. I am indebted to him.

Thanks to Marcus Gadau, Ph.D.
More than anyone else Marcus Gadau has been instrumental in the refinement and dissemination of MPD education in both the US and Europe. He has tirelessly worked to clarify our unique method from the vast offering on www.doane.us to the conception and development of this book. I am honored to have a practitioner and intellect of his caliber among my most loyal students and cherished colleagues.

Thanks to Adi Korman, L.Ac.
Adi Korman is responsible for the final editing and overall professional tone of the book. Adi trained as a resident in my clinic for 2 years. He is currently working for Modern Acupuncture in Scottsdale, Arizona.

Thanks to Hayden Hennington, L.Ac.
I would like to give special thanks to Hayden Hennington for organizing the first chapters of this book. Hayden is an accomplished MPD practitioner and has worked behind the scenes as an organizer to bring this book to publication.

Foreword

It is an extreme honor for me to write the foreword for this book. Bob and I first met seventeen years ago at an acupuncture seminar. From that first encounter, I was impressed with his explanation of how acupuncture works by stimulating different types of nerve fibers, the spinothalamic tract and other pathways. As a physician trained in western medicine first, I had never once thought about bringing modern physiology and neuroscience into the field of TCM. Instead, I had always embraced the concepts of Qi, the meridians, the five elements, etc. With the same innovative, integrative and forward-thinking approach, Bob has learned and re-analyzed TCM pulse diagnosis, becoming a master practitioner and a world-class teacher in this field.

There is a tendency for practitioners in allopathic, naturopathic, chiropractic and integrative medicine to hand out prescription drugs or to advise nutritional supplements based on patients' diagnosis and/ or subjective complaints. This approach is referred to by some as "match the pill to the ill." For example, with stomach complaints, proton pump inhibitors (PPIs) such as Nexium or Prilosec are frequently prescribed, but not every patient benefits from PPIs. If the pulse at the right Guan position is weak, the clinical implication would be that there is no hyperacidity or acute inflammation and the patient is better treated with digestive tonifying herbs. It was a little difficult for me to grasp the concept "treat the pulse, don't mind the diagnosis" in the beginning. However, I now fully understand the wisdom in that statement. I now use pulse diagnosis to guide my herbal treatments and have seen tremendous results over several years. As another example, back home in Taiwan, when patients complain of fatigue, they often expect some sort of Qi-boosting herbs from Chinese Medicine doctors. If the practitioner is not proficient in pulse diagnosis and goes along with the patients' request, the outcome could be detrimental such as extremely high blood pressure or increased risk of stroke.

I have made several trips to Bob's clinic and attended his workshops and webinars in the past several years. Bob has improved his teaching materials and the current book represents the newest and most illustrative version summarizing his knowledge and experience on this topic. It should be easy for the readers to appreciate different pulse patterns at different locations because of the excellent graphic representations. With Bob's endeavor and the advent of this pulse diagnosis manual, TCM practitioners will move to a higher level of expertise. Syndrome differentiation finally becomes easy. Patients become better, faster, and the practitioners confidence and professional satisfaction improves.

When I work as a clinical oncology professor teaching fellows in outpatient cancer clinics, I often show them how to read patients' pulses and how to use the pulse pattern as a quick and useful guide to someone's body constitution. It is my dream that one day the pulse examination taught by Bob will become part of physical diagnosis taught at every US medical school. As the entire medical profession is quickly replacing palpation, percussion and auscultation with blood tests and imaging studies, physicians should still keep some simple yet accurate hands-on diagnostic skill such as Chinese Medical Pulse Diagnosis.

Confucius once reminded his disciples that if they failed to work hard and forgot how to perform ceremonial rituals, they might have to go to other countries to learn in the future. I will say the same to TCM doctors in Taiwan and China. If they do not study hard and if they ignore pulse diagnosis, one day they may have to go to Poulsbo, Washington, U.S.A. to learn from Bob.

Peter Sheng, M.D. O.M.D.
Clinical Professor (Volunteer)
Division of Hematology-Oncology
University of Cincinnati Medical School
Cincinnati, OH.
U.S.A.

Preface

You are practicing a millennia-old, honorable and invaluable medical system, as relevant now as it was two thousand years ago. You have invested years of your life and extensive resources to learn how to use this medicine to help people and to create a fulfilling career for yourself. As an outsider to the mainstream medical community, your skill using this medicine (and not your titular status) determines your success. This skill and other specifics of your practice also influence the growing understanding of this medicine's scope, safety, and effectiveness. This is a daunting task that requires a tremendous amount of knowledge, guidance, and grit. And, sadly, far too many practitioners of this medicine are failing. They are unable to financially support themselves with their practice because they can't produce predictable and repeatable positive results for their patients.

Pause right now and ask yourself: "Do my clinical results live up to the potential I know exists within this medicine? Do my patients benefit from this medicine's unique ability to restore healthy function?"

If the honest answer to these questions is "NO," do not despair. You are not alone, and there is a remedy. In the following pages, I outline in precise detail a tried-and-true method of quickly diagnosing and effectively treating (see soon to be published volume two) nearly every patient that walks into your clinic. This method is rooted in Chinese Medical theory but takes into account the complexity of modern-day patients and a current physiological understanding of the body. I know this system works because I've used it with hundreds of thousands of patient visits in one of the busiest Chinese Medicine clinics in the United States for the past twenty years. I humbly believe it is the most effective pulse diagnostic system taught in the world today, and every year, I share this knowledge with Chinese Medicine practitioners and MDs in dozens of countries around the world. For the first time, I am presenting the MPD method in book format to reach all the practitioners who need it. Whether you are newly embarking on a career in this medicine or looking to advance an existing practice, the tools in this book will elevate your use of Chinese Medicine to the status it deserves.

Robert Doane, L.Ac., 2018

Introduction

It is clear that the majority of Chinese Medicine practitioners lack confidence in their ability to correctly diagnose and treat patient illness in the clinical setting. For most, this is not due to a lack of intelligence or motivation, but rather an educational approach that insufficiently develops the diagnostic skills necessary to navigate complex patient cases. Students training in Chinese Medicine learn the traditional examination skills of inquiry, inspection, listening, and palpation. Conventional instruction implies that the information gathered by each of the clinical examinations should lead to a single differential diagnosis. In clinical practice, these particular examination findings often conflict with one another, and the nuance required for effective treatment is lost in findings that are overly generalized (e.g. 'a weak pulse'). The practitioner is overburdened with theory and resorts to the clinically inefficient approach of focusing on patient symptoms. This approach is one of the main obstacles to effective clinical diagnosis and treatment. Strictly following patient reportings perpetuates the diagnostic mistakes that have prevented the majority of Chinese Medicine practitioners from achieving the superlative effects of this medicine. All practitioners need effective diagnostic skills to navigate the clinical setting and treat complex patient cases. With dedicated practice, Medical Pulse Diagnosis (MPD) will rapidly increase your skill and success in the field of Chinese Medicine.

A vast amount of diagnostic information is gathered through proper pulse diagnosis. The common practice of pulse diagnosis is implemented superficially to verify a predetermined diagnosis or tacitly disregarded as inconclusive due to other diagnostic findings. Many practitioners were erroneously taught to believe that mastery of pulse diagnosis requires decades of learning or even the endowment of mystical and esoteric knowledge. Other endeavoring practitioners get lost in the disorganized and incomplete historical literature that presents isolated pulse pictures with no clear connection to treatment. Other dedicated pulse diagnosticians have developed the ability to deduce pathology, but lack clinically effective methods to treat these pulse findings. Pulse diagnosis and effective treatments can be learned and implemented systematically. After many years of learning and refinement through the experiences of a high-volume patient practice, I am sharing what I believe is the most effective pulse diagnostic system.

In this book, I will share the precise details of my unique system for determining the diagnosis of patient conditions. I will teach you how to develop the tactile sensitivity as well as the systematic logic that will guide correct pulse diagnosis and effective patient care.

Succeeding texts will focus thoroughly on the precise treatment strategies and herbal prescriptions used clinically to address each pulse presentation. A principal focus will be on the continuous supervision of patient cases necessary for maximal long-term resolution. This text applies to all Chinese Medicine practitioners and provides clinical value to any biomedical healthcare practitioner seeking palpable insights into patient conditions. These methods have produced diagnostic accuracy concerning the health of over 30,000 patients and 500,000 patient visits over the last twenty years. My goal is to contribute this same level of diagnostic expertise to your clinical practice and your patients.

MPD Goals of Volume 1

1. Learn MPD pulse positioning for reliable pulse diagnosis

2. Learn locations of all MPD pulse positions

3. Learn the anatomical correspondences of MPD pulse positions

4. Learn the healthy pulse presentation for each MPD pulse position

5. Learn the five pulse Depths

6. Learn the pathological High and pathological Low pulses

7. Learn the pathological Forceful and pathological Forceless pulses

8. Learn the pathological Thick and pathological Thin Pulses

9. Learn the pathological pulses based on combination of Shape, Depth, Force, and Width

10. Learn the treatment strategies for each pathological pulse combination

I

Brief History of Chinese Pulse Diagnosis

As with many aspects of Chinese Medicine, details of the development of pulse diagnosis are obscured by its long history and incomplete written record. Many textual sources simply did not endure into the 20th century, as highlighted in reference works that are unknown to the western reader (Hammer, 2016). Also, the historical reliance on experiential instruction and use of linguistic tools (such as songs or poems) over a comprehensive written record, leaves only a partial picture of the historical discovery and use of this tool. The earliest historical references trace pulse diagnosis to the 5th century BCE and the practices of a physician named Bian Que, though none of his works are extant (Hsu, 2010). Starting with the Huang Di Nei Jing and spanning the past two millennia, there have been a series of milestone works on the pulse that either elaborate upon or disagree with the previous works. From these, the standard TCM view of pulse diagnosis was derived. Although the MPD system deviates significantly from this standard practice, understanding the broad chronicles of the literary history is beneficial. What follows is a review of these major works and their contribution to pulse diagnosis, as well as the contemporary practices that have influenced the development of MPD.

Huang Di Nei Jing (黃帝內經) [Yellow Emperor's Inner Canon]

The Huang Di Nei Jing [Yellow Emperor's Inner Canon], compiled between 100-300 BCE, describes circulation of blood (Xue) and vital air (Qi) throughout the body. It defines the normal pulse as a pulse rate of four beats per breath circuit, with pulse rates above or below this level signaling pathology. The pulse is used along with facial color to assess the severity of disease, particularly impending death or the capability of recovery (Darmananda, 2000). A number of different pulse-taking sites on the head, neck, and limbs were described, presumably drawn from different practices in use at the time. One method explains how to assess the functional state of the acupuncture vessels by palpating the superficial arterial pulse attributed to each of the twelve vessels. However, some of these pulses would only be palpable in pathological conditions. Three pulses - the carotid, radial, and dorsalis pedis arterial pulses - are emphasized by virtue of being palpable in the healthy and diseased patients. The Huang Di Nei Jing was the first text to correlate regions of the radial pulse with the functional state of specific internal organs (Walsh, 2008).

Nan Jing (難經) [The Classic of Difficulties]

The Nan Jing [The Classic of Difficulties] was compiled during the first century CE by an unknown author, though it is sometimes associated with Bian Que. "Following the Sung era, it was misidentified as merely an explanatory sequel to the Yellow Emperor's Inner Canon. This volume, however, demonstrates that the Nan Jing should once again be regarded as a significant and innovative text in itself" (Unschuld, 1986). The Nan Jing concludes that there is a single interconnected circuit of blood circulation in the body carrying vital physiological materials throughout the organism. By this unified circulation concept, the individual pulse positions were considered to reflect the totality of the human body. This was the first significant emphasis on the primary use of pulse palpation in patient diagnosis. It specifically promoted the Cun Kou, radial artery, as the optimal pulse assessment site for practical and theoretical reasons. In different sections of the text, it divides the three positions of the radial artery into two, three, and five depths (Flaws, 2006).

The Works of Zhang Zhong Jing (張仲景)

The famous author of the Shang Han Lun (傷寒論) [On Cold Damage] and Jin Gui Yao Lue (金匱要略) [Essential Prescriptions of the Golden Cabinet] included numerous mentions of pulse findings in his early third century CE texts. Zhang Zhong Jing emphasized the importance of corroborating the pulse with the dominant signs and symptoms to make an accurate diagnosis. In this way, pulse presentations were part of the defining features of six Yin and Yang levels of etiology and pathology. Limited details were given about each pulse, though he advised taking the pulse at multiple sites for complex conditions (Morris, 2011).

Mai Jing (脈經) [The Pulse Classic]

In addition to reorganizing the Huang Di Nei Jing, Wang Shu He authored The Pulse Classic, which is the oldest extant book solely dedicated to the description of the radial pulse findings. It relied heavily on the theory of etiology, stages, and progression of disease described in the preceding Huang Di Nei Jing, Nan Jing, and works of Zhang Zhong Jing. It discusses at length the use of pulse diagnosis as a prognostic tool for patients' imminent death or potential recovery from various infectious diseases common at the time. This differs from much of modern day pulse practice, which aims to assess the nature of non-emergent health issues. The Mai Jing describes the location and organ correlation of the three positions on each wrist, twenty four different complex pulse images, and alterations in the pulse due to season and constitution. This work provides lengthy discussions on various pulse qualities but does not clarify the complete process of palpation, diagnosis, and treatment. Most notably, it supports the two-level system that couples Yin-Yang paired organs in each position, placing the Yang organ superficially and the Yin organ at depth. This understanding persists to this day. The Mai Jing's somewhat cryptic descriptions invited many published interpretations in the centuries that followed (Shu-Ho, 2002).

Bin Hu Mai Xue (瀕湖脈學)

Li Shi Zhen composed the Bin Hu Mai Xue in the 16th century as a summation of all extant pulse writings and specifically an elaboration of the material in the Mai Jing [The Pulse Classic]. This concise work was written in short rhyming phrases to aid memorization. It is divided into two sections; the first describes the pulse physiology and the second elaborates on Wang Shu He's specific pulse images. This text differs from the Mai Jing in that it ascribes one Yin organ to each position and describes three depths of pressure that reflect the Qi, Blood, and Yin aspect of each organ (Hammer, 2012). The Bin Hu Mai Xue was and still is an influential theoretical book, often serving as a primary influence for contemporary pulse diagnosticians.

John Shen and the Ming He lineage

From the 20th century to the present day there have been many noteworthy lineages of pulse diagnostic knowledge, some of which exist as published works and others that have passed along family or disciple lineages. The medical, cultural, and political developments of 20th century China are relevant to the teachings of Dr. John Shen and Dr. Zhang Wei Yan (Dr. Jimmy Chang), both influential in the development of MPD.

Dr. John Shen learned from the influential Ding Gan Ren and the Ming He lineage, which dates back to the early 17th century CE. This method was known as the "Ming He" current, named after the town in eastern Jiangsu province where it originated. Ding Gan Ren wrote a pulse diagnosis book called "Summary of Pulse Study" that is unavailable in English, which incorporated Li Shi Zhen's work with other noteworthy pulse diagnosticians.

Much of Dr. John Shen's life and educational background are unknown, but he undoubtedly studied the classics thoroughly and built his treatment principles and herbal formulas alongside the theories of Chinese Medicine. He was, perhaps, the earliest doctor to practice pulse diagnosis in the United States in a significant manner. Notably,

Dr. Shen used unique descriptions of pulse findings that revolved around biomedical systems and diagnoses. The cardiovascular system and nervous system were particularly important in many different primary etiologies of disease (Hammer, 2016).

I studied Dr. Shen's methods for approximately 3 years. A number of the pulses in my system bear the same or similar names to Dr. Shen's system; however, my finger positions for the cun, guan, and chi pulses are completely different from those taught by Dr. Shen. The Shen system is a brilliant integrative method and has had a significant impact on the practice of Chinese Medicine.

Dr. Zhang Wei Yan (Dr. Jimmy Chang)

The Taiwanese practitioner, Dr. Jimmy Chang, developed a unique and practical set of pulse theories and terms that identify predictable deviations from a defined normal pulse at each pulse position. His main book on pulse diagnosis is Pulsynergy - A Pulse Diagnosis Manual. Though well-versed in the classics of pulse diagnosis, he considers much of the historical information to be overly complicated and inflexible when treating complex patient presentations. He believes reliance on the standard practice of traditional pulse diagnosis tends to prioritize memorization over clinically focused critical thinking. This, in turn, limits the usefulness of pulse diagnosis in efficiently determining patient treatment (Chang, 1995). He has operated a busy herbal clinic in Los Angeles, CA for decades where he sees thirty plus patients daily, affording him a considerable sample size to refine his pulse interpretations. He has been actively teaching in the United States for over two decades through the Lotus Institute of Integrative Medicine and designs many of the herbal formulas for Evergreen Herbs.

Dr. Chang has had the most significant influence on the development of MPD. I studied with him for approximately 10 years. His pulse diagnosis, in my opinion, is the best there is. Over the course of many years and hundreds of thousands of treatments MPD was born. Significant changes to the Chang method occur in the cun position. MPD's finger positioning for the cun is different and more accurately reveals problems with Heart functioning. MPD also places much more importance on the role of Blood Stasis and its pulse identification.

Wang Qing Ren (王清任)

In my review of historical contributions to MPD, a word must be said about the work of Wang Qing Ren. His 1830 book, Yi Lin Gai

Cuo (醫林改錯) [Correcting the Errors in the Forest of Medicine], deepened Chinese Medical understanding of the pivotal role of the circulatory system in health and disease. Frustrated with the contradicting descriptions of anatomy throughout the Huang Di Nei Jing and Nan Jing, he voraciously sought firsthand knowledge of the visceras shape and anatomical placement, as well as the size and distribution of blood vessels in the torso. Through extensive (post-mortem) anatomical study and clinical application, he developed a group of herbal formulae focused on blood stasis that remains indispensable in clinical practice to this day (Neeb, 2006). Over the past twenty years of intensive clinical experience and modern biomedical knowledge, I have come to many similar conclusions as Wang Qing Ren. My approach to diagnosis and treatment stems from my clinical observations of Blood Stasis as a primary etiology of many diseases. I much admire his insight and willingness to contradict conventionally held medical views. I am indebted to his contribution to Chinese Medicine.

It was not until the modern era that novel terms and pulse position correlations became associated with modern biomedical knowledge. The traditional approach to pulse diagnosis is the memorization of the twenty-four to twenty-eight classical pulse images coupled with prolonged study of traditional Chinese Medical theory. With years of study and clinical experience, it is believed that the practitioner will develop the skills to interpret the pulse for diagnosis of disease progression and effective treatment strategies. However, the study of these elaborate pulse pictures does not offer a systematic and complete method for interpreting the radial pulse. Clinically, a practitioner is capable of perceiving various pulses which do not conform to the particular classical pulse categories. Also, practitioners may observe multiple traditional pulse categories simultaneously in individual patients.

These issues lead the majority of Chinese Medicine practitioners, in both China and abroad, to abandon reliance on this valuable diagnostic tool. The continuation of this book aims to transmit a coherent and systematic approach for pulse diagnosis that has guided hundreds of thousands of effective treatments for twenty years.

2

Cardiovascular Review

Learning MPD and translating our findings into effective treatment strategies requires a comprehensive understanding of biomedical knowledge. It is imperative that the MPD practitioner has an appreciable comprehension of the anatomy and physiology of the cardiovascular system, as well as western medical approaches to diagnosis and treatments.

Palpation of the radial pulse, in specified MPD positions, highlights distinguishable rheological features that can inform the practitioner of the patient's health conditions. This system yields considerable health insight regarding most anatomical regions including specific organ systems, musculoskeletal issues and the overall condition of the vascular system. The ability to relate cardiovascular features with corresponding pulse presentations is a valuable tool for the clinical practitioner.

The MPD system emphasizes the cardiological influence in many common pathologies, as well as complicated disease manifestations. Over many years, MPD has categorized refined pulse presentations of the left Cun position representing the functionality of the heart. Classical Chinese Medicine distinguishes the heart as the 'Emperor' organ, emphasizing its principal physiological role in the maintenance of physical health. The millennia-old detailed descriptions of the vascular system and the specific substances of systemic circulation instruct the effective clinical practice of Chinese Medicine.

The nature of the heart organ and its influence on the entire body is remarkable. The heart organ beats on average 60-80 times per minute, about 100,000 times per day and about 35 million times per year. The entire vascular system is approximately 60,000 miles in length and circulates nearly 5-6 liters of blood three times a minute, totaling 2000 gallons of blood circulated each day (Cleveland Clinic, 2016). In the following cardiovascular review, significant features of anatomy and physiology, diagnostics and pathology, and common allopathic treatments are the focus. The scope of this book relates to both the Chinese medical and western medical knowledge most relevant to the MPD method. Advanced information and medical research emerge continually, and I highly recommended that all practitioners refer to biomedical and cardiology publications for continuing education.

I. Anatomy and Physiology

Structure and Position

Approximately the size of one adult fist, the heart sits asymmetrically marginally left of the chest's midline, anterior to the esophagus and between both lungs. Its numerous vascular connections are located behind the second intercostal space, while the heart apex rests on the diaphragm near the fifth intercostal space. The fibrous, multi-layered pericardium encases the heart muscle anchoring its position between the lungs and serves to lubricate and protect the heart from infection.

Chambers and Valves

The heart accommodates four chambers, two atria above (right and left) and two ventricles below (right and left). The atria are smaller in dimension, and need to circulate sufficient quantity of blood into the ventricles. The left ventricle, tasked with commencing systemic circulation, has thicker musculature than the right. Each ventricle contains an inlet and outlet valve whose proper coordination ensures that the ventricles efficiently move the blood along a unidirectional path. The four valves and their positions are the tricuspid valve (R atrium → R ventricle), pulmonary valve (R ventricle → lungs), mitral valve (L atrium → L ventricle), and aortic valve (L ventricle → whole body). The valves are two-cusped (mitral) or three-cusped (tricuspid) structures that open and close. The tricuspid and mitral valves possess tendinous and muscular tethers which prevent backflow of blood against the intense pressure of the ventricles. The valves are anchored to the fibrous cardiac skeleton to support the proper closure.

Artery Anatomy

Recognizing subtle details when palpating the radial artery highlights physiological information related to various regions of the body. The radial pulse is a defined segment of the vascular system, which interconnects and sustains all body tissue and organ systems. Understanding the structure of arterial tissue helps in the interpretation of the radial pulse variations perceived clinically.

Both the heart and the arteries are composed of three layers that share a similar function. The outer adventitia, or tunica externa, is primarily composed of collagen and serves to anchor and protect the artery. The middle layer, tunica media, is composed of smooth muscle, which can dilate or constrict to affect blood pressure. Both vasodilation and vasoconstriction occur in response to the autonomic nervous system and circulating hormones. The tunica media is enclosed by an elastic membrane, which influences the arterial walls to rebound slightly with each pulsation of the heart. This rebound tension helps to prevent dramatic blood pressure fluctuations between ventricular contractions and also adjusts for elevated heart rate upon exertion. The elastic nature of the arterial system tends to diminish with age.

The innermost tunica intima is made of endothelial cells and creates a smooth surface for efficient blood circulation through the arteries. Due to lower blood pressure, the veins have thinner walls compared to arteries and incorporate valves to maintain the unidirectional flow of blood against gravity.

In an adult, the diameter of the blood vessels ranges from over an inch in the aorta (about the width of a garden hose), to about 5 microns in the capillaries (about 1/10 the width of a human hair). The capillaries maintain the essential function of material exchange within the body. The human body has about 1 billion capillaries, and no cell in the body is more than 60-80 microns away from a capillary (Saladin, 2004).

Electrical Conduction of the Heart

The sinoatrial (SA) node triggers the heart rate (sinus rhythm). This specialized neural tissue is located along the muscular wall of the right atrium and serves as a natural pacemaker by spontaneously depolarizing. The higher rate of the sinoatrial node is maintained between 60-80 bpm by the vagus nerve of the parasympathetic nervous system. Activation of the sympathetic nervous system response, induced by increased serum epinephrine/norepinephrine levels, causes the heart rate to temporarily rise above these levels until the vagus nerve reestablishes the normal sinus rhythm. These cardiac mechanisms of the autonomic nervous system are regulated by the cardiac center of the medulla oblongata.

The electrical impulse from the sinoatrial (SA) node passes along a specific pathway to the atrioventricular (AV) node and is transmitted between the ventricles to trigger ventricular contraction. This critical impulse is kept from spreading outside of its normal pathway or beyond the heart by the insulating effect of connective tissues within the heart muscle and the outer lining of the heart and pericardium.

Stroke Volume and Ejection Fraction

The volume of blood that the heart can pump with each contraction, called the stroke volume, is dependent on the following factors. Preload is the volume of blood in the ventricles before they contract, and afterload is the pressure in the vascular system that the left ventricle will be pushing against. Contractility is the relative strength of the myocardium to eject stroke volume. The percentage of total blood volume of the ventricles that is forced out is called the ejection fraction and equals 55%-75% for the average patient.

Circuit of Blood

Blood flow is functionally divided into pulmonary circulation and systemic circulation, each driven by the motive force of the respective right and left ventricle. Pulmonary circulation follows the path: R ventricle – pulmonary valve – pulmonary arteries – lungs (alveoli) – pulmonary veins – L atrium. At this point, systemic circulation commences: Mitral valve – L ventricle – aortic valve – aorta – arterial circulation – capillaries – venous circulation – vena cava – R atrium – tricuspid valve. The 5-6 liters of blood in the human body completely circulate this course three times per minute, traveling more than 12,000 miles per day. The heart organ itself has very high demands for nutrient and oxygen and receives blood supply via two main coronary arteries branching off the root of the aorta. The coronary veins return deoxygenated blood supply into the R atrium.

Rheology and Contents of Blood

Blood is a type of connective tissue that contains an extracellular matrix (plasma) that supports and organizes living cells (red and white blood cells). It can also be defined as an organ because it has a structure, contains living cells, and has specific functions. In addition to RBCs (transporting dissolved oxygen) and WBCs, the blood circulates platelets, lipids, hormones, vitamins, minerals, antibodies, sugars, clotting factors, and proteins. Similarities exist with the millennia-old language of Chinese Medicine, which describes Xue (blood) to carry Qi (vital air), Ying (nutrients), Wei (defensive substances), and Jing (vital organ substances) to all of the body tissues (Kendall, 2002).

Blood circulates among varying pressure gradients within the vascular system and does not operate as a standard Newtonian fluid. For example, blood viscosity reduces as an adaptation to the increased pressure at peak systole. This particular adaptation is termed the shear rate. The specific risk factors associated with cardiovascular disease also appear to have a systemic influence on blood viscosity. The risk factors include high blood pressure, elevated low-density lipoprotein (LDL) cholesterol, lowered high-density lipoprotein (HDL) cholesterol, type-II diabetes, metabolic syndrome, obesity, smoking, and aging (Lowe, 1997). There is reason to believe that increased blood viscosity is the only biological parameter linked with all of these major cardiovascular risk factors.

The functional descriptions of increased blood viscosity share many features with the Chinese Medicine concept of Blood Stasis. This essential topic will be described thoroughly in later chapters concerning specific pulse findings and clinical treatments. Though subjective, the MPD practitioner palpates valuable diagnostic information based on the relative 'thinness,' 'thickness,' or 'smoothness' of the blood circulating within the radial artery. These trained palpatory skills translate into more accurate and nuanced diagnosis and directed treatment.

2. Cardiovascular Pathology

Cardiovascular disease (CVD) is responsible for approximately one-third of all deaths worldwide. In the United States, someone dies every 39 seconds from a cardiovascular event. Cardiovascular and cerebrovascular treatments account for one in six medical dollars spent, approximately $300 billion each year (American Heart Association and Center for Disease Control). Cardiovascular disease is a global health crisis.

The majority of healthcare practitioners fail to recognize the signs and symptoms of pre-clinical cardiovascular disease. CVD may develop over decades and in the worsening stages can compromise the quality of life. These patients often suffer from a reduced sense of overall vitality and may experience concurrent health conditions. From both the biomedical and Chinese Medicine perspective, many common health complaints relate to compromised vascular function. The skilled MPD practitioner can detect the signs related to cardiovascular decline and provide directed treatment that can improve this overall condition. The practice of Chinese Medicine demonstrates a cardiovascular focused approach that can fill a crucial role in the prevention of this healthcare crisis.

Common General Symptoms

As with other medical disciplines, patient interviewing and observation assessments are pillars of the Chinese Medicine examination. However, clinical dependency solely on patient reporting and biomedical diagnosis can detract from effective treatment results. The clinical practice of MPD can establish efficiency in the diagnostic process, limiting reliance on exhaustive symptom reporting, and serving as the primary diagnostic tool. In conjunction with MPD, practitioners need be aware of the symptoms described below. These symptoms commonly signal the compromised functioning of the cardiovascular system. The analysis of these symptoms can be helpful in practicing effective herbal therapy, and at times are crucial for identifying emergent conditions that demand a referral to a primary care physician (PCP) or emergency department.

Fatigue: Reduced blood supply to the muscular system can induce weakness, fatigue, and cramping. Fatigue is one of the most common clinical symptoms and can express as a result of many pathologies. Ask the patient to gauge the degree in which the fatigue limits their activities and overall quality of life.

Shortness of breath (SOB): Outside of respiratory conditions such as asthma, allergies, and infections, this symptom can manifest with nervous system disorders, coronary artery disease, and heart failure. Commonly, the more advanced heart pathologies will induce SOB with the least amount of physical activity.

Palpitations: One of the most common symptoms seen in the ER is one that 15% of all people experience in a given year. Palpitations are defined as unpleasant sensations of irregular and/or forceful beating of the heart. It is difficult to identify the cause of palpitations if they occur paroxysmally. Often, this symptom is considered benign, unless symptoms are lasting, severe, or repeatable (see red flag section below). In Chinese Medicine, palpitations and associated symptoms are diagnosed and treated accordingly.

Chest pain: This symptom may express due to various issues of the pulmonary system, cardiovascular system, musculoskeletal system, and upper digestive tract. With a focus on heart pathologies, chest pain may result from a prolapsing mitral valve (often defined and sharp pain), vasospasms of the coronary arteries or atherosclerosis of the coronary arteries causing heart ischemia, pericarditis, and aortic dissection.

Limb Pain: Numbness, fixed or paroxysmal pain symptoms indicate either reduced blood circulation to the limb due to cardiac insufficiency, systemic blood vessel constriction, or a blood vessel obstruction by an embolus.

Skin color & swelling: Pallor, cyanosis, or redness of limbs or face. The cause of these symptoms depends on the complete presentation. These symptoms may signal reduced perfusion to the skin, due to numerous factors, and local or systemic inflammation. Edema of the lower legs or lower back is often related to heart pathology or potential deep vein thrombosis. Enlarged neck veins, especially with the patient at a 45-degree tilt, often correlates with congestion of the R atrium.

Lightheadedness or fainting (syncope): Commonly related to a reduced cardiac output or sudden temporary drop in blood pressure. The carotid arteries branching from the aortic arch depend on adequate blood pressure to fulfill the high blood, oxygen and nutrient demands of the brain. The causative factors of these symptoms are often valvular issues that affect blood pressure or the vasovagal response caused by stress.

Changes in Consciousness

Chinese Medical theory describes the heart as the 'seat' of the animating spirit or individual consciousness. In the clinical setting, it is imperative to observe the emotional qualities of our patients. This tool provides valuable insight into how each patient responds to their environment and highlights the health of the heart. This observation, corroborated with pulse findings, leads the practitioner to more effective treatments of the whole person. From a Chinese Medicine perspective, the particular symptoms of anxiety, hypervigilance, forgetfulness, lack of clarity and disturbed sleep relate to specific aberrations of the heart.

Red Flag Referrals

The MPD practitioner may be in a position to detect a potentially dangerous pulse finding that demands referral to a PCP or emergency care. Tachycardia of greater than 100 bpm (beats per minute) with concurrent nervousness or hypervigilance (or apathy in the elderly) and heat aversion with warm skin can indicate undiagnosed hyperthyroidism. If the heat and agitation are pronounced, there is a potential for 'thyroid storm,' a life-threatening condition (Anzaldua, 2010).

Additionally MPD practitioners may encounter patients with palpitations. Palpitations are a common subjective experience that does not necessarily correspond with an arrhythmia but can signal a severe or emergent condition. A general rule for referral is as follows: recent onset palpitations, or those that accompany lightheadedness, numbness, tingling, or chest pain, or occur during exercise merit a referral (Anzaldua, 2010).

Common Cardiovascular Diagnoses

Considering the systemic role of the cardiovascular system, any minor tissue or mechanical dysfunctions can produce amplified systemic effects over time. Cardiovascular dysfunctions can be sufficiently categorized as valve issues, rhythm issues, arterial narrowing or blockage, heart muscle compensation, and changes in the viscosity or pressure of the blood. Below are the most common diagnoses and a brief description. Many of these issues occur concurrently.

Arrhythmias: Any deviation from the normal heart rate and rhythm, ranging from benign to life-threatening. Premature atrial arrhythmias may result in bradycardia, bradyarrhythmia, supraventricular tachycardia (SVT), atrial fibrillation, or atrial flutter.

Cardiomyopathy: An enlargement, stiffening, or thickening of the heart muscle, compromising the heart's capacity to circulate blood.

Arteriosclerosis: The thickening, hardening and loss of elasticity of the arterial vessel walls. This process gradually restricts the blood flow to the various organ and tissue systems of the body.

Atherosclerosis: A narrowing of the arterial lumen by a combination of accumulated lipids, proteins, cholesterol, calcium, inflammation and the proliferation of vessel cells resulting in reduced blood circulation along the arterial distributions. This condition can lead to coronary artery disease, peripheral artery disease, carotid artery disease, aneurysms and chronic kidney disease.

Heart Insufficiency and Congestive Heart Failure: Any of the pathologies that result in inefficient pumping of blood by the heart muscle.

Valve issues: Weakness or rigidity causing incomplete closure or prolapse of the cardiac valves. These issues lead to regurgitation of blood within the heart and are diagnosable as heart murmurs, graded on a scale of one to six.

Hypertension (HTN): Sustained elevated arterial pressure which can contribute to conditions such as heart disease, stroke, and vision loss. 90-95% of cases are primary (essential) HTN and are related to to unknown lifestyle or genetic causes. Secondary HTN accounts for the remaining 5-10% and is the result of specific illness or medication.

Hyperlipidemia: Elevated serum lipid levels, especially LDL (low-density lipoprotein) cholesterol.

Myocardial Infarction: The sudden life-threatening necrosis of heart tissue due to occlusion of the coronary arteries in patients with Coronary artery disease (CAD).

Common Diagnostic Testing: Patients that have received bio-medical treatment for cardiovascular issues will likely have undergone one or more of the common procedures described below. Each procedure has inherent strengths and weaknesses.

X-Ray: Shows the location, size and shape of the heart, lungs and the blood vessels.

ECG/EKG: Informs on the electrical conduction of the heart. The ECG/EKG is an initial diagnostic procedure to diagnose arrhythmias, an infarction in progress, pericarditis, enlargement of the heart, electrolyte imbalances, and drug-induced effects on the heart. Often, a Holter Monitor is used during a Stress/Treadmill Test to induce an observable event or analyzed for a 24-hour (or longer) period.

Echocardiogram: Evaluates cardiac chamber size, wall thickness, valve functioning, blood flow in the chambers and the ejection fraction.

Cardiac catheterization (Angiogram): The catheter is threaded through the femoral artery to the cardiac region. A radioactive dye is injected, and X-ray images of the heart are taken for analysis of the heart condition and coronary vessels. This procedure is the "gold standard" for the evaluation of coronary artery disease.

Standard Cardiac Stress Test: A twelve lead ECG, blood pressure device and pulse oximetry measures the heart's ability to respond to external stress in a controlled clinical environment. The test is performed to evaluate patient symptoms and a wide range of dysfunction including arrhythmias, cardiac ischemia, exercise tolerance, oxygen consumption and congenital or valvular heart disease.

Myocardial Perfusion Imaging (MPI): Examines blood circulation through the heart during exercise on a treadmill or exercise bicycle and while resting.

The test uses a radioactive material called tracers that mix with the blood and circulate to the heart muscle. A specialized camera images the heart to show how well the heart muscle is perfused (supplied with blood). Results determine narrowings or blockages of the coronary arteries or previous tissue damage due to myocardial infarction.

Coronary Calcium Scan: Analyzes the potential build-up of calcium, or calcifications, as a sign of atherosclerosis, coronary heart disease, or coronary microvascular disease. A coronary calcium scan will determine an Agatston score that reflects the amount of calcium found in the coronary arteries. A score of zero is normal, and higher levels correlate with the increased risk of heart disease.

Blood testing: Analysis of high levels of enzymes that indicate heart muscle damage, blood lipids, inflammatory markers (C-reactive protein, etc.), and electrolytes, among other substances.

3

12 Steps to Accurate MPD Positioning

The development of MPD as presented in this text is the result of twenty years of high volume clinical experience. The unique discoveries and cardiovascular emphasis of this method come from continuously observing the same pulse signs and concurrent symptoms in thousands of patients. Modern medical research continues to support the clinical observations of MPD.

Clinical knowledge pervades the ensuing chapters, which cover the most efficient MPD clinical procedures and relevant diagnostic information. The MPD system and novel herbal strategies are continually evolving toward greater clinical success for the patient. Every day in the clinic is an opportunity for continued learning through patient observation and treatment experimentation. This method provides every practitioner with the fundamental tools to thoroughly investigate the patient's physiology and related symptoms. With continuous clinical practice, MPD will lead to further medical discoveries that contribute to the effectiveness of Chinese Medicine.

Accurate Diagnostic Positioning

The MPD pulse positions designate precise anatomical regions on the radial artery. Positional variations have been taught in both ancient and modern pulse diagnostic methods, generating inconsistencies and confusion for most practitioners. The MPD pulse positions differ from most traditional pulse teachings and provide an advanced standardization of pulse locations for accurate diagnosis. The following instruction serves to guide the practitioner in each essential step of the MPD process.

Clinical MPD proficiency is dependent on a systematic course of action. The following 12 steps outline the fundamental methods for accurate diagnostic positioning. Included in these descriptions are the common "pitfalls" that compromise the efficient practitioner and patient positions. The fulfillment of these 12 steps is essential for all further MPD diagnostic actions. With clinical experience these steps will become second nature in the pulse taking process.

Step 1 - Introduction & The Upright Hand

The optimal MPD position is with the patient sitting directly across from the practitioner. Having a desk or table, at approximately diaphragm level, between the patient and practitioner is ideal for both sides to remain comfortable and obtain proper positioning.

Upon first meeting, the patient is directed to sit across from the practitioner and place their hands comfortably on the table, similar to a handshake position.

It is best to describe the MPD process with new patients. Below is an example:

"I know this may be foreign to you, but there is over 2000 years of empirical evidence for this diagnostic method. Chinese Medicine is the oldest, still practiced medical system in the world with many generations of doctors having refined the system. The process of pulse diagnosis is related to simple fluid dynamics. As blood travels down your forearm, in the radial artery, it bounces against the bone at the wrist, called the scaphoid bone. This event creates a slight backflow of blood and a resulting wave-pattern. Chinese doctors discovered thousands of years ago that these wave-patterns correspond to certain changes in various regions of the body, and developed a refined diagnostic method."

During the MPD process, it is recommended to start with the analysis of the right-side radial pulse, then followed by the left-side radial pulse. Place the patient's right hand in an upright, "gravity-neutral" position. Take their right-side pulse with your left hand - from this point called the diagnosing hand - as shown in figure 1. Diagnose the left-side pulse with the right hand. Ensure that the diagnosing hand approaches the patient's hand from the dorsal aspect, not from the ventral aspect (figure 1).

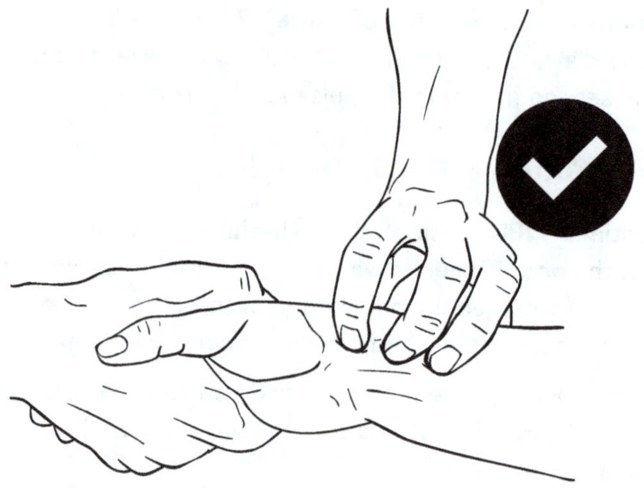

Figure 1: The patient's right hand is in an upright position

Step 1 - Pitfall #1: Patient's Hand Presents
in the Supine Position

Do not take the pulse in this position (figure 2), as it will flatten the radial pulse due to gravity. This position also torques the radial artery and tenses adjacent structures such as tendons (e.g., flexor carpi radialis tendon) and ligaments (e.g., palmar carpal ligament).

Figure 2: Incorrect position of patient's hand lying in the supine position

Step I - Pitfall #2: Pulse Taken From Patient's Ventral Side

Do not analyze the pulse with the diagnosing hand coming from the patient's ventral side (figure 3). This position inevitably leads to muscular forearm tension in the patient, as the diagnosing hand has no anchoring point. The position also makes it difficult to assess pulse depths accurately.

Figure 3: Incorrect position of practitioner's hand approaching from the ventral side

Step I - Pitfall #3: Pulse Diagnosis With Patient's Palm Facing Upward And Diagnostic Hand Coming From Ventral Side

Figure 4 demonstrates an entirely ineffective way of analyzing the radial pulse in the MPD system. The patient's hand in the supine position and the diagnostic hand approaching from the ventral aspect both disrupt the proper diagnosis. This pulse diagnosis position is the standard in TCM textbooks.

Figure 4: Incorrect patient hand position and the practitioner's diagnostic hand approaching from ventral aspect

Step 2 - Stabilize The Patient's Hand

Stabilize the patient's hand with a gentle, relaxed handshake (figure 5). The practitioner's hand performing this action is called the stabilizing hand. The stabilizing hand allows the practitioner to gauge and maintain the tensional state of the patient's arm. If the patient's arm is not relaxed, it is essential to prompt the relaxed state. This state is often achieved by removing the diagnosing hand and patting the patient's hand or forearm in a friendly manner.

The stabilizing hand is essential for maintaining the MPD diagnostic position for the duration of the diagnosis. With compromised stabilization, the patient will often flex the wrist joint, which obscures the Cun position and distorts the radial artery.

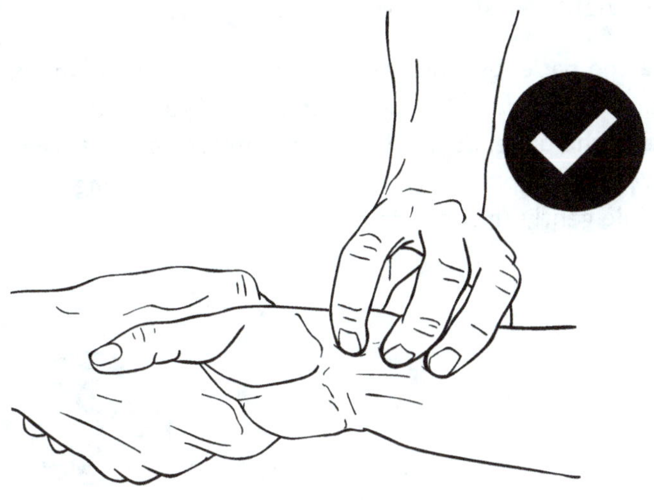

Figure 5: Stabilizing hand holds patient's hand

Step 2 - Pitfall: Holding Only The Fingers of Patient's Hand

It is improper to both hold the patient's fingers (figure 6) or envelop the patient's entire hand (including the thumb) with the stabilizing hand during the pulse diagnosis. Both situations will cause tension of the flexor carpi radialis tendon and other periarticular structures surrounding the radial artery.

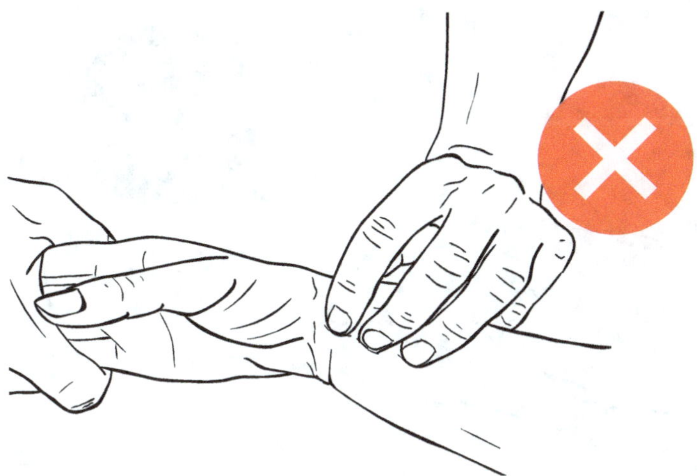

Figure 6: Practitioner only holds the fingers of the patient

Step 3 - Straight Wrist Relaxed Forearm

Ensure the patient's hand, and arm both align in an anatomically neutral position, neither flexed or extended (figure 7 & 8). It is also essential that the patient's hand and forearm are relaxed. The practitioner can promote proper relaxation by verbally cueing the patient to relax while gently shaking the hand.

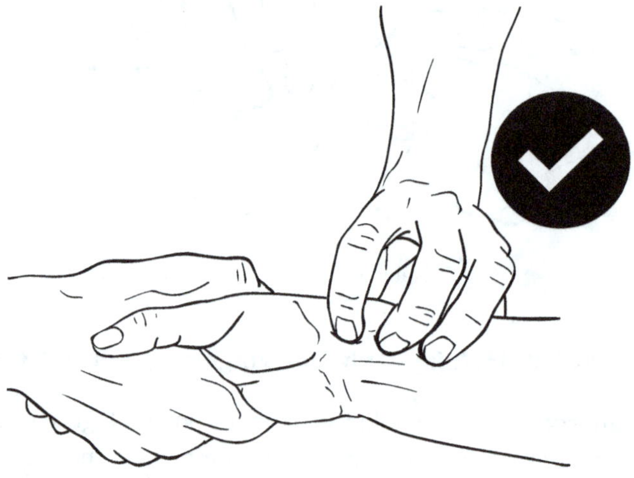

Figure 7: Correct position of the patient's hand and arm and the practitioner's hands

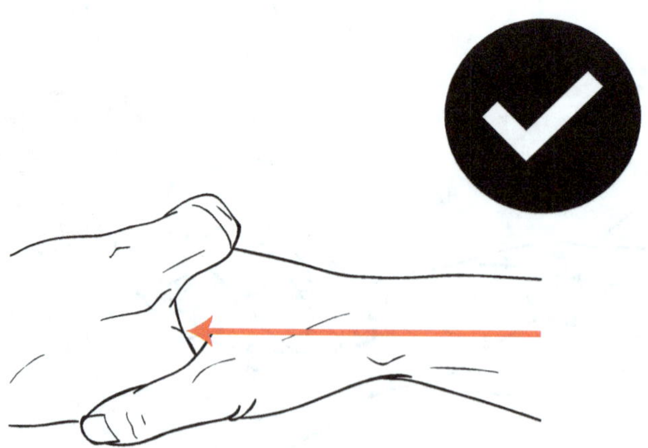

Figure 8: Correct position of the patient's hand and arm
and the practitioner's stabilizing hand

Step 3 - Pitfall: Unintended Flexion or Extension of Patient's Hand

Even slight flexion (figure 9) or extension (figure 10) will put tension on the periarticular structures adjacent to the radial artery. Flexion minimizes the Cun position, while extension elevates the radial artery to the superficial skin level. An important reason for the practitioner to sit directly opposite, or to the side of the patient, is to mitigate these positional issues that distort the MPD analysis.

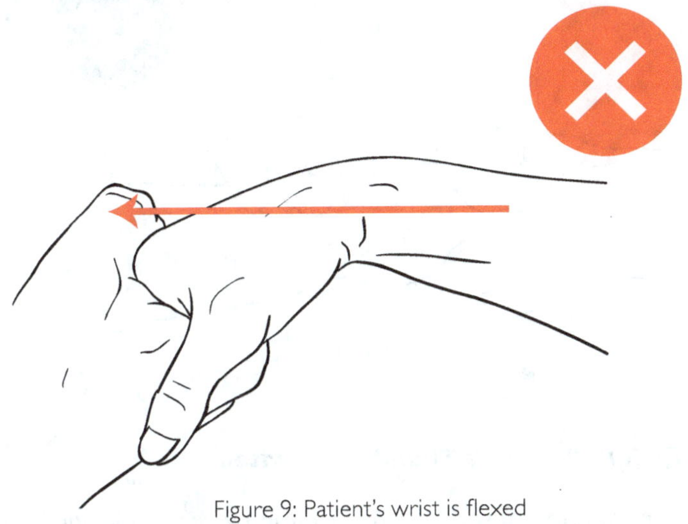

Figure 9: Patient's wrist is flexed

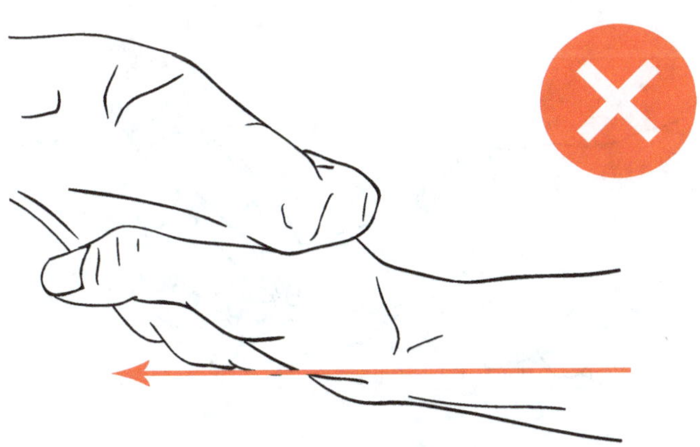

Figure 10: Patient's wrist is overextended

Step 4 - Patient's Thumb Down and Relaxed

Ensure that the patient's thumb is relaxed (figure 11). Patients often engage a "thumbs up" position, intending to be helpful (figure 12). This position contracts the tendons of the abductor pollicis longus and extensor pollicis brevis, obscuring the Cun position.

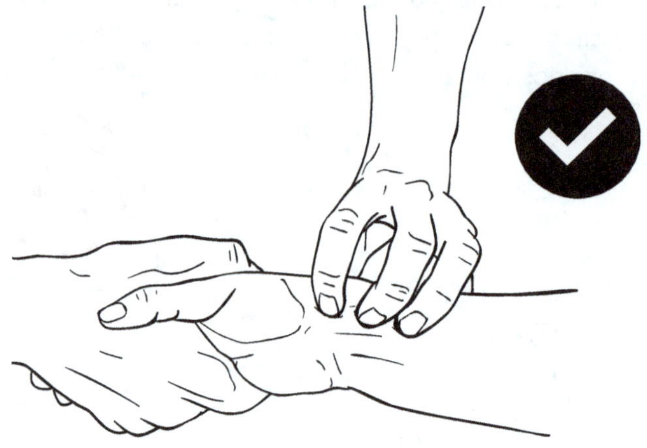

Figure 11: Patient's thumb is relaxed

Step 4 - Pitfall: Patient's Thumb is Elevated

Ensure relaxation of the patient's thumb by gently placing it in the relaxed position.

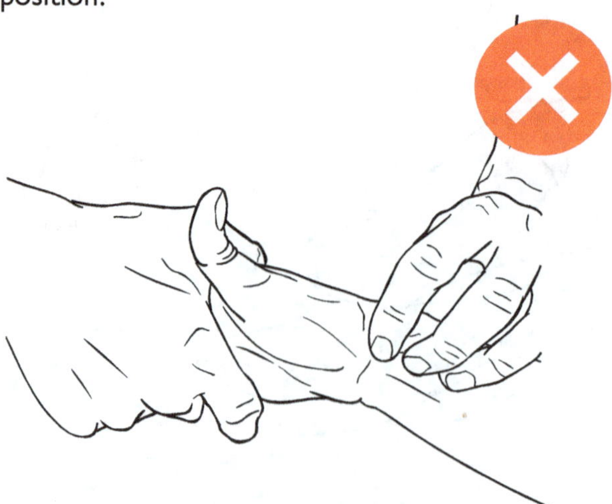

Figure 12: Patient's thumb is elevated

Step 5 - Anchor Thumb of the Diagnostic Hand

Anchor the thumb of the diagnostic hand securely on the dorsal aspect of patient's wrist in the region of acupoint Yang Chi, SJ4 (figure 13). This positioning promotes the alignment of the diagnosing fingers over the correct pulse positions. The thumb anchor also provides leverage to facilitate the relaxed pressure necessary when palpating the pulse depths.

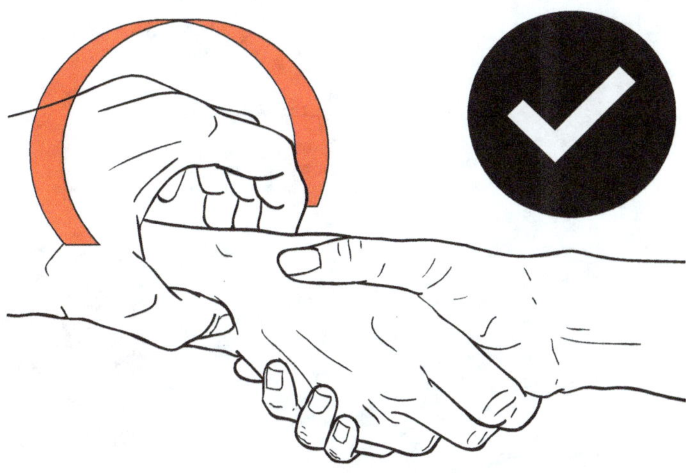

Figure 13: Diagnosing hand correctly anchored by the thumb

Step 5 - Pitfall : Absent/Incorrect Anchor

Two mistakes are common during this essential step. One mistake is altogether failing to incorporate the diagnostic hand's thumb as an anchor (figure 14). The second mistake is utilizing the diagnostic hand's thumb as an inefficient semi-anchor by resting on the anatomical snuffbox (figure 15). With these mistakes, there is an absence of anchoring force on the dorsal aspect of the patient's forearm to oppose the pressure of the diagnosing fingers. The patient's arm will deviate upon palpation of the deeper levels of the radial pulse and distort the complete diagnosis.

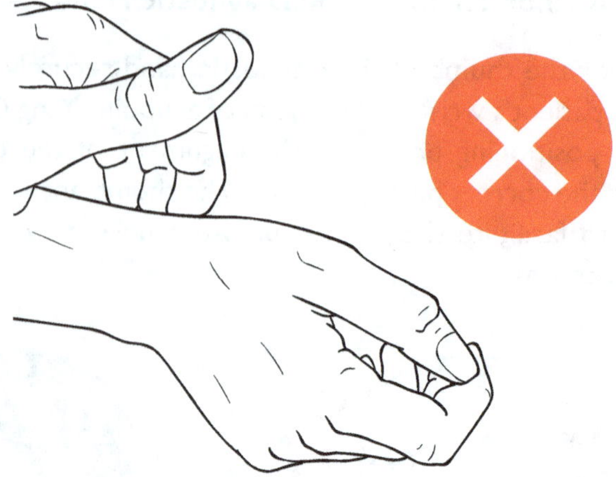

Figure 14: Practitioner's thumb is not anchored

Figure 15: Practitioner's thumb is incorrectly anchored

Step 6 - Egg-Shaped Diagnosing Hand

The correct MPD diagnostic position requires rounding the diagnostic hand to produce an "egg-shaped" posture (figure 16). This posture promotes a relaxed position for the diagnostic fingers with proper flexibility and mobility for palpating the various pulse positions. This posture also places the center of the finger pads at a 45-degree angle on the radial artery (figure 17). The center of the finger pads provides the highest level of tactile sensitivity during the diagnosis.

Position all three fingers (index, middle and ring finger) on the radial artery and palpate the individual pulse positions with one finger at a time. In the initial MPD learning stages, the practitioner is most suited to using the diagnostic hand's index finger for palpating the pulse positions. The index finger pad is superior in tactile sensitivity and remains the essential asset for even the experienced MPD practitioner.

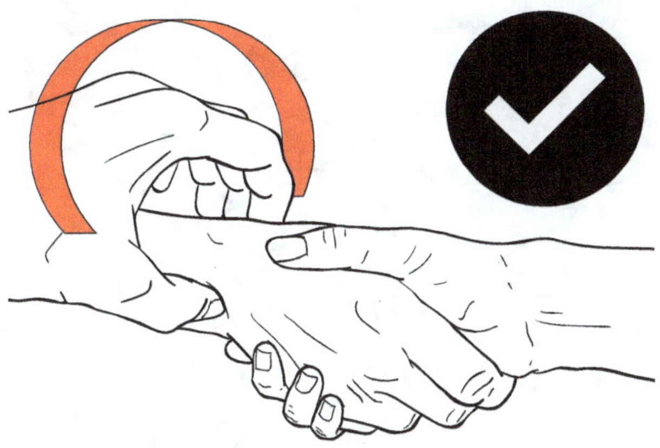

Figure 16: Diagnosing hand is in "egg-shaped" position

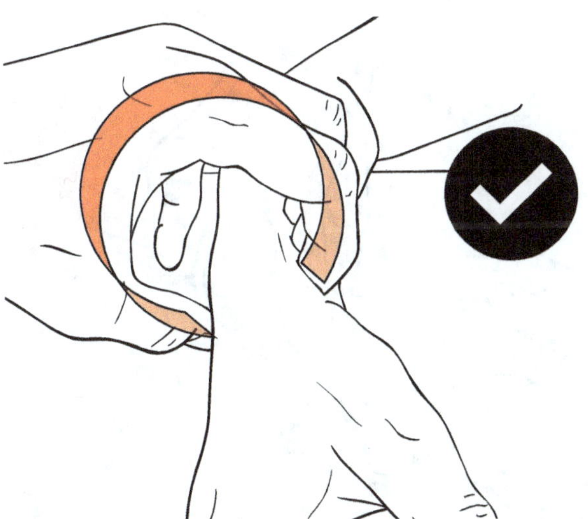

Figure 17: Center of finger pads at a 45-degree angle on the radial artery

Step 6 – Pitfall #1: Incorrect Angle

Figures 18 and 19 illustrate the same incorrect angle of the fingers for MPD analysis. This 80-90 degree angle places the maximal distal portion of the finger pads on the pulse. A lack of tactile sensitivity will compromise the diagnostic procedure.

Figure 18: Incorrect angle of diagnostic fingers

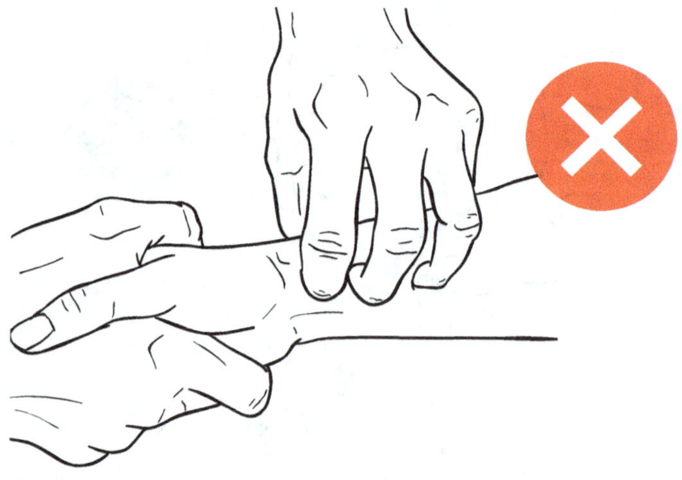

Figure 19: Incorrect angle of diagnostic fingers

Figures 20 and 21 illustrate a collapsed finger pad placement on the radial artery. This displaces the center finger pad from the proper positions, thus compromising tactile sensitivity for appropriate diagnosis.

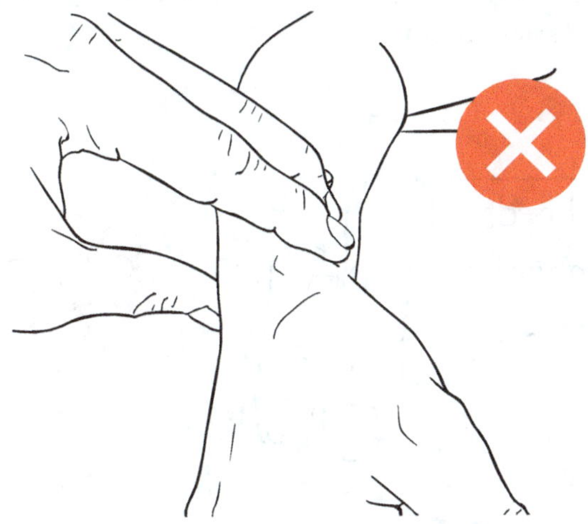

Figure 20: Incorrect angle of diagnostic fingers

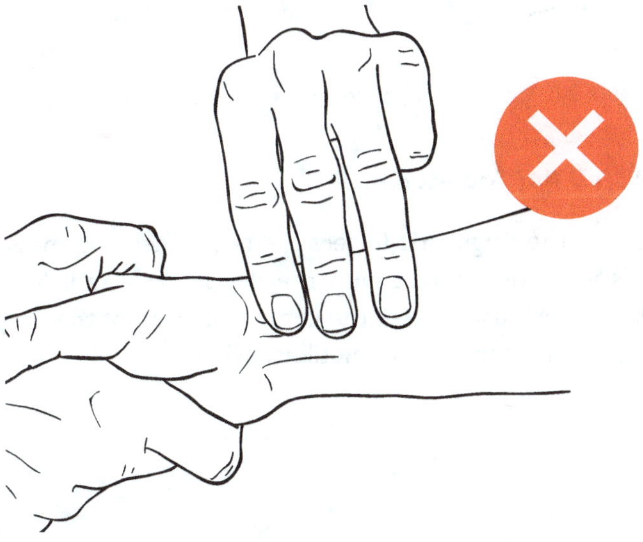

Figure 21: Incorrect angle of diagnostic fingers

Step 6 - Pitfall #3: Exaggerated Pressure

Figure 22 illustrates the most common error executed by novice MPD practitioners. The application of excessive pressure is easily identified by the diagnostic finger-nail beds turning white. This level of pressure occludes the radial artery and decisively negates the pulse analysis. As described in later chapters, each pulse position requires analysis of five distinct depths.

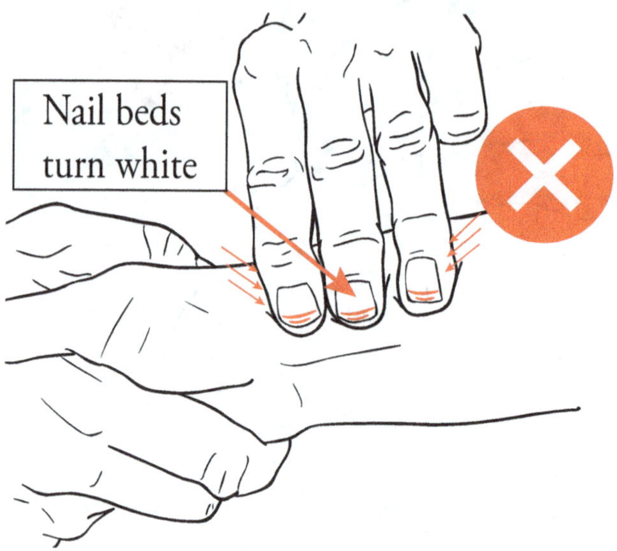

Figure 22: Applying exaggerated pressure on the radial artery

Step 6 - Pitfall #4: Too Medial

Ensure that the diagnostic fingers are not placed too medially on the patient's wrist, in contact with the flexor carpi radialis tendon (figure 23). As previously noted, the central portion of the diagnostic finger pads provides the correct tactile sensitivity.

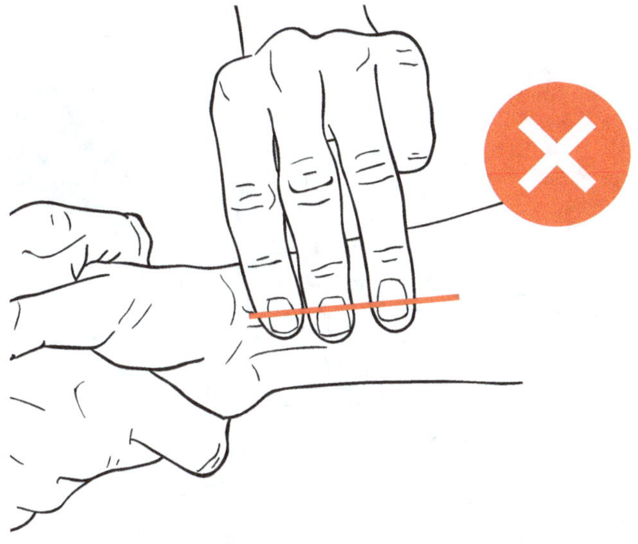

Figure 23: Finger pads placed too medial to the Cun, Guan and Chi positions

(Red line indicates the flexor carpi radialis tendon)

Step 7 - Landmark - The Styloid Process

The first essential step to identifying the proper MPD positions is to locate the radial styloid process. With each patient, locate the styloid process by gently palpating from distal to proximal along the radius at the wrist joint. The radial styloid is the anatomical landmark utilized in every MPD analysis to differentiate the location of the Cun and Guan positions. Once located, place the index finger in the anatomical indentation located between the scaphoid bone and the distal end of the styloid. This entire region is termed the Cun "valley," containing the proper Cun position and additional identifiable pulse positions. The styloid process serves as the partition between the Cun and Guan regions. Place the middle finger slightly proximal to the proximal end of the styloid to locate the proper Guan position. Spreading the index finger and middle finger on either side of the styloid process is termed "gapping" the styloid process (figure 24).

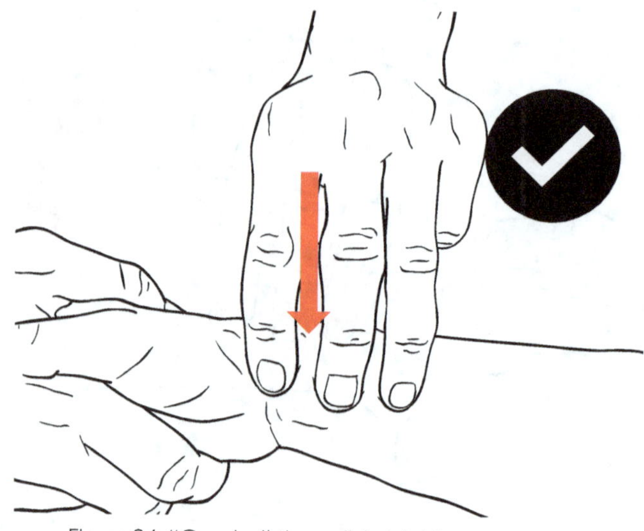

Figure 24: "Gapping" the radial styloid process

Step 7 - Pitfall: Not Gapping The Styloid Process

The Cun position is distal, and the Guan position is proximal to the radial styloid process. Do not confuse the styloid process region with either of these pulse positions. Figure 25 illustrates this critical positional mistake.

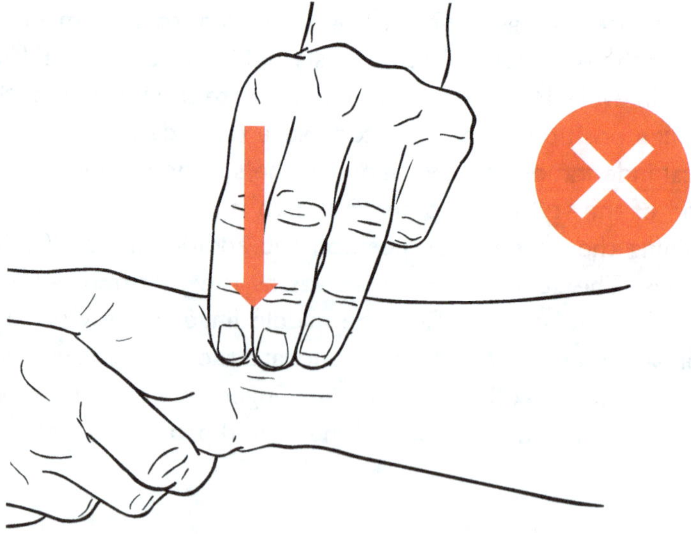

Figure 25: Not "Gapping" the radial styloid process

Step 8 - The Cun "Valley"

The precise identification of the Cun "valley" is a requisite step for effective MPD practice and clinical success. Locate this region between the proximal end of the scaphoid bone and the distal end of the radial styloid process.

The Cun "valley" region accommodates five separate pulse positions. Each of the five pulse positions corresponds to distinct arterial vessel features of this anatomical region.

Yin Wei Pulse (figure 26):

In most individuals, the radial artery first bifurcates in the region of the radial styloid process. The medial branch termed the superficial palmar arch follows the lateral border of the flexor carpi ulnaris tendon. This pulse position represents the Yin Wei pulse.

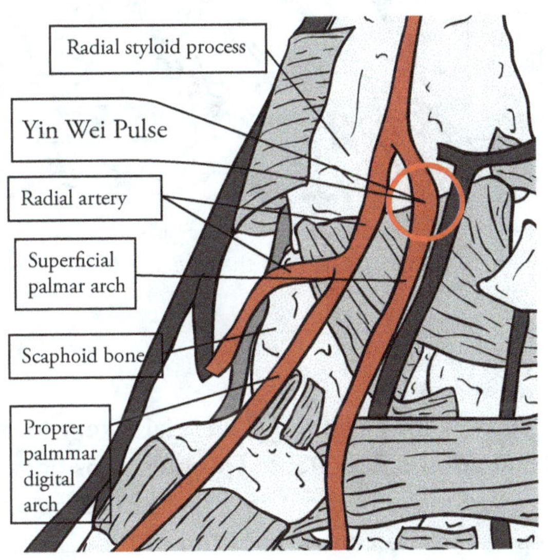

Figure 26: Yin Wei pulse
(Anterior view, radial aspect of the forearm at wrist crease)

Yang Wei Pulse (figure 27):

The Yang Wei pulse is distinguished by the second, and more distal, bifurcation of the radial artery. At this location, the radial artery bifurcates into the proper palmar digital arch (central) and the continuation of the radial artery (lateral). The lateral continuation of the radial artery is the Yang Wei pulse.

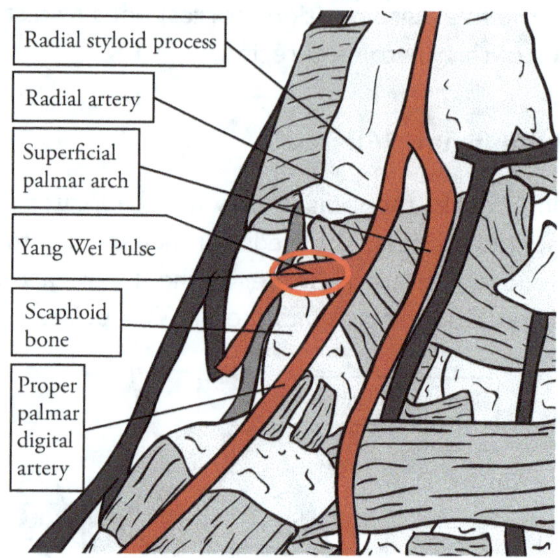

Figure 27: Yang Wei Pulse
(Anterior view, radial aspect of the forearm at wrist crease)

Cun Pulse (figure 28):

The Cun pulse is the region of the radial artery located between the proximal and distal bifurcations. This pulse positions centrally between the Yang Wei pulse (lateral) and the Yin Wei pulse (medial). Locate the Cun pulse in the central location of the Cun "valley" region between the proximal scaphoid bone and the distal styloid process.

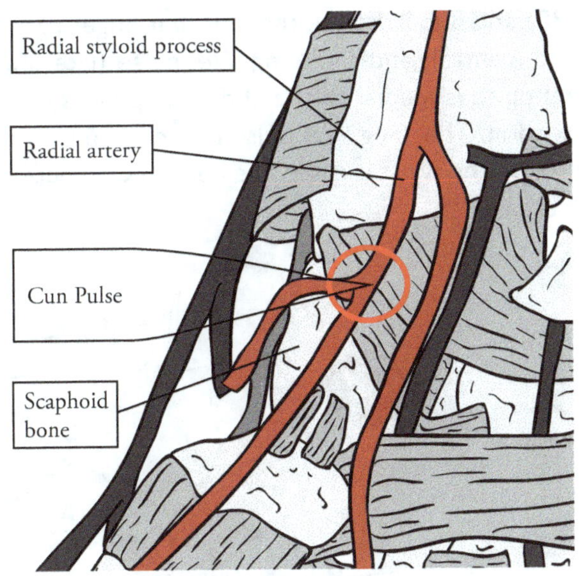

Figure 28: Cun Pulse
(Anterior view, radial aspect of the forearm at wrist crease)

Figures 29a and 29b illustrate the different finger pad locations of the Cun pulse (central) and the Yin Wei pulse (medial). For proper palpation of the Cun Pulse, the index finger is rotated 30-40 degrees distally towards the patient's scaphoid bone. This essential technique is described at the end of Step 8. The Yin Wei pulse is palpated medial to the Cun position, adjacent to the flexor carpi radialis tendon. For palpating the Yin Wei pulse, the index finger pad is positioned perpendicularly, with no finger pad rotation.

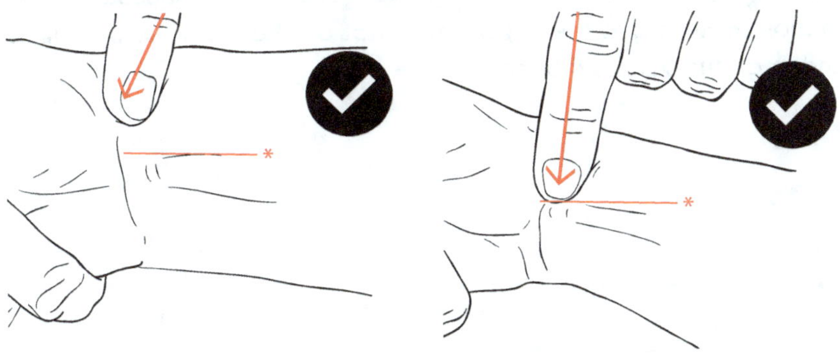

Figure 29a: Cun Pulse

Figure 29b: Yin Wei Pulse

(*Flexor carpi radialis tendon)

Figures 30a and 30b illustrate the different finger pad locations of the Cun pulse (central) and the Yang Wei pulse (lateral). Note that the Yang Wei pulse is medial to the abductor pollicis longus tendon, not on the tendon. The Yang Wei pulse is lateral and slightly distal to the Cun pulse, on the wrist crease. The central Cun pulse is proximal to the wrist crease.

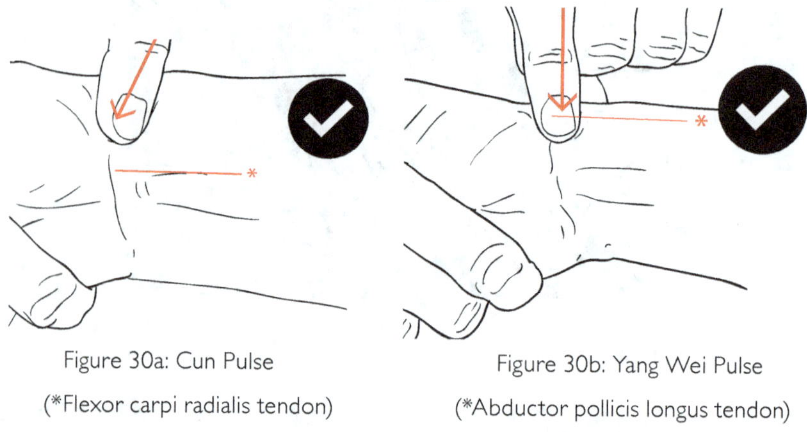

Figure 30a: Cun Pulse

(*Flexor carpi radialis tendon)

Figure 30b: Yang Wei Pulse

(*Abductor pollicis longus tendon)

Large Vessel Pulse (figure 31):

The Large Vessel pulse is located distal to the Yin Wei pulse on the same superficial palmar arch. This pulse is precisely situated at the wrist crease junction of the superficial palmar arch, the flexor carpi radialis tendon, and the scaphoid bone. In patients with relevant pathologies, a compressed pen-tip like pulse will be palpable at this junction. Ensure that the finger pad is not on the flexor carpi radialis tendon or the scaphoid bone.

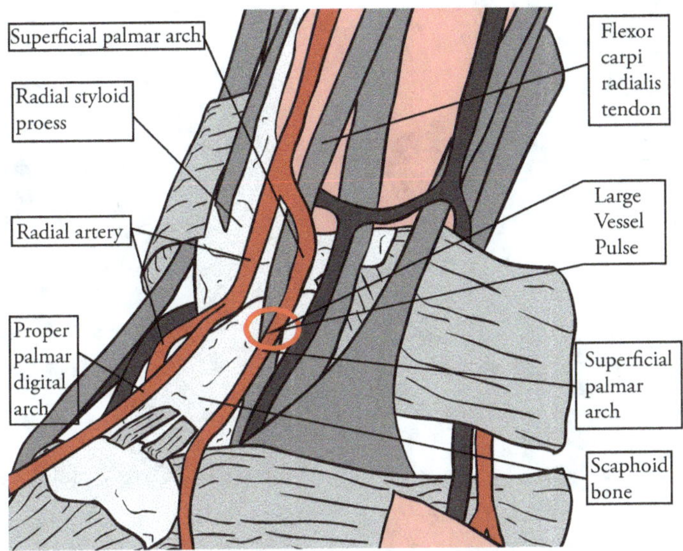

Figure 31: Large Vessel Pulse
(Anterior view, radial aspect of the forearm at wrist crease)

Figures 32a and 32b illustrate the different finger pad locations of the Large Vessel pulse (distal) and the Yin Wei pulse (proximal). Note that the Yin Wei pulse is proximal to the wrist crease and the perpendicular position of the index finger upon palpation. The Large Vessel Pulse is at the wrist crease, and the index finger pad is rotated slightly toward the patient's scaphoid bone to analyze this junction.

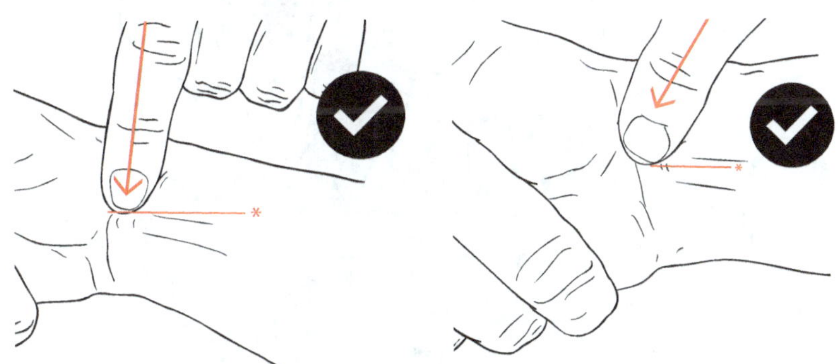

Figure 32a: Yin Wei Pulse   Figure 32b: Large Vessel Pulse

(*Flexor carpi radialis tendon)

Figures 33a and 33b illustrate the different finger pad locations of the Cun Pulse (central) and the Large Vessel pulse (medial).

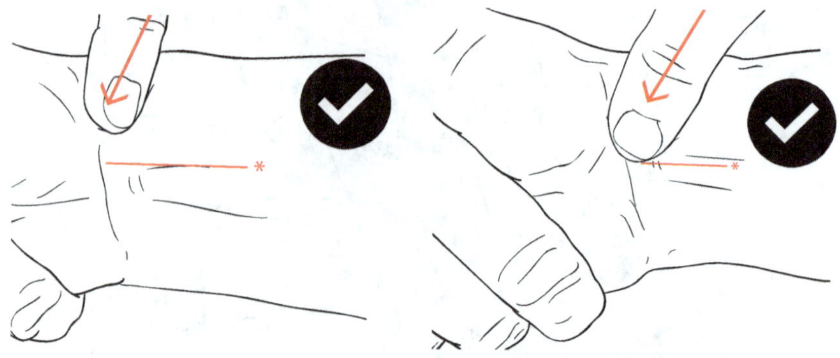

Figure 33a: Cun Pulse   Figure 33b: Large Vessel Pulse

(*Flexor carpi radialis tendon)

Mitral Valve Pulse (figure 34):

The Mitral Valve pulse location is most lateral of all Cun region pulses. The lateral branch of the radial artery (same as Yang Wei Pulse) continues in the lateral direction, under the tendons of the abductor pollicis longus and extensor pollicis longus. In specific valve conditions, a distinct pulse can be palpable on the top of the abductor pollicis longus tendon.

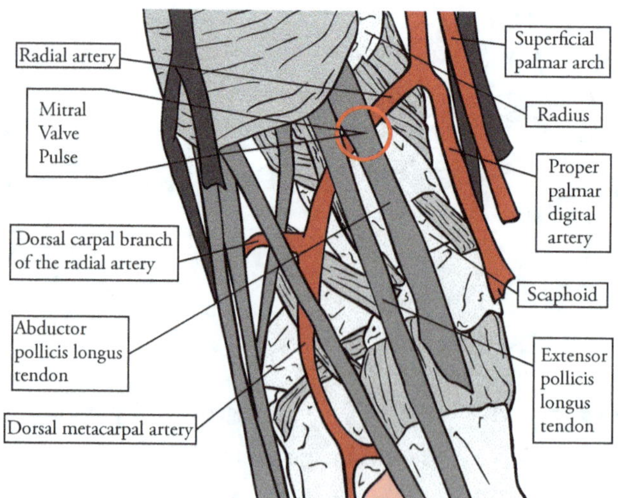

Figure 34: Mitral Valve Pulse
(Radial-lateral view, radial aspect of the forearm at wrist crease)

Figure 35 illustrates the proper location and palpation of the Mitral Valve pulse. The Mitral Valve pulse is assessed on the left side. Place the index finger pad on top of the abductor pollicis longus tendon with light pressure which can then be gradually increased. The lateral radial artery can be palpated on the top of the abductor pollicis longus tendon in the presence of heart valve conditions. It is important to note that the mitral valve pulse is not due to the finger coming in direct contact with the lateral radial artery since that artery is underneath the tendon. Consequently, if a pulse is felt on the top of the abductor pollicis longus tendon, it is due to the strong pulsation of the artery underneath the tendon making the tendon pulsate as if there was an artery on top of the tendon. Both the lengthy history of anecdotal evidence and personal clinical experience have verified the correlation between the Mitral Valve pulse and general heart valve conditions (dominantly mitral valve). The presence of this pulse on the right side may be indicative of a valve problem, either of the tricuspid valve or the pulmonary valve. More research is needed in this case.

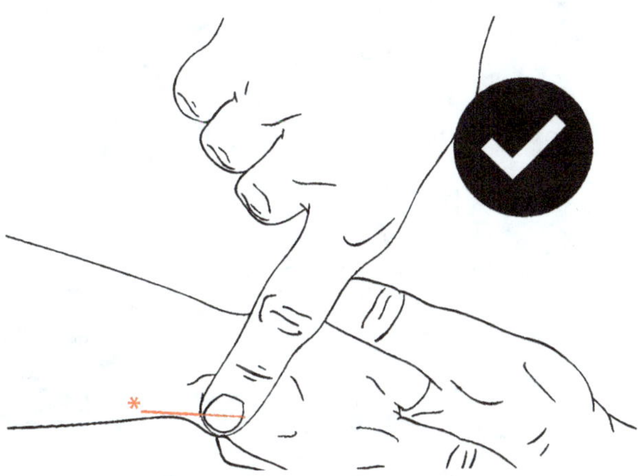

Figure 35: Palpating the Mitral Valve Pulse
(*Abductor pollicis longus tendon)

Palpation of the central Cun pulse is unique to all other pulse positions. First, position the index finger pad in the center of the Cun "valley," between the proximal scaphoid bone and the distal radial styloid process. Next, reposition the diagnostic hand's thumb anchor from the wrist region of acupoint SJ 4 to the middle of the dorsal side of the patient's hand (figure 36). This positioning promotes the alignment of the diagnosing index finger over the Cun position. Following the anchor thumb's reposition, rotate the index finger 30-40 degrees toward the patient's scaphoid bone (figure 37). This adjustment places the central finger pad in the distinct Cun pulse position. A common MPD error is misinterpreting the distal radial styloid pulse for the Cun pulse. The rotation of the index finger is the essential step for correctly palpating the Cun pulse and averting the separate distal styloid pulse.

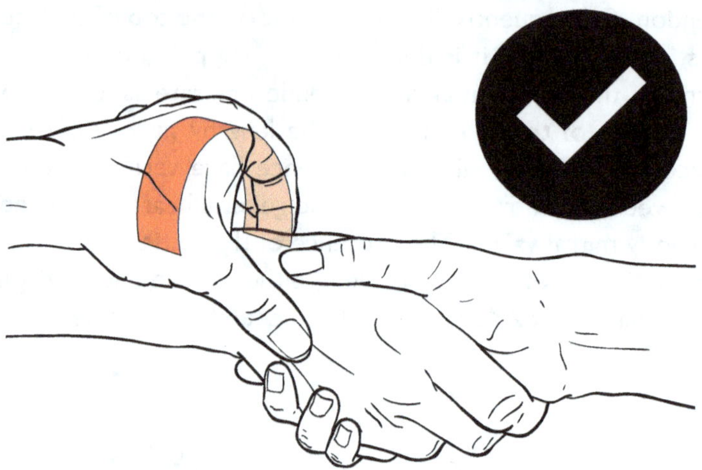

Figure 36: Reposition of thumb anchor from the wrist region to hand region

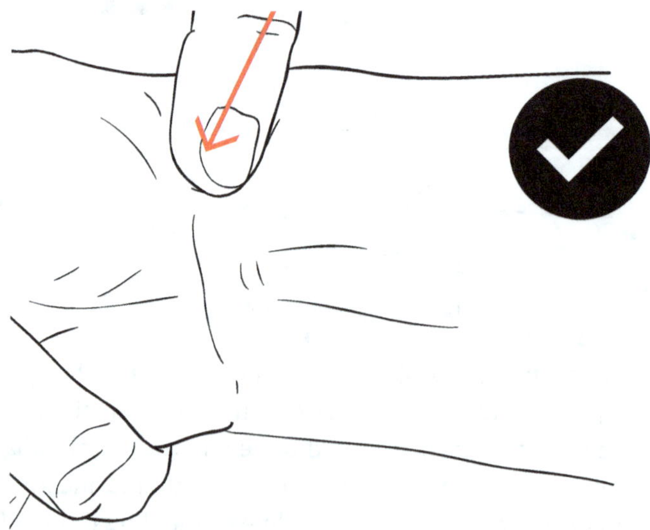

Figure 37: Rotated index finger when palpating the Cun Pulse

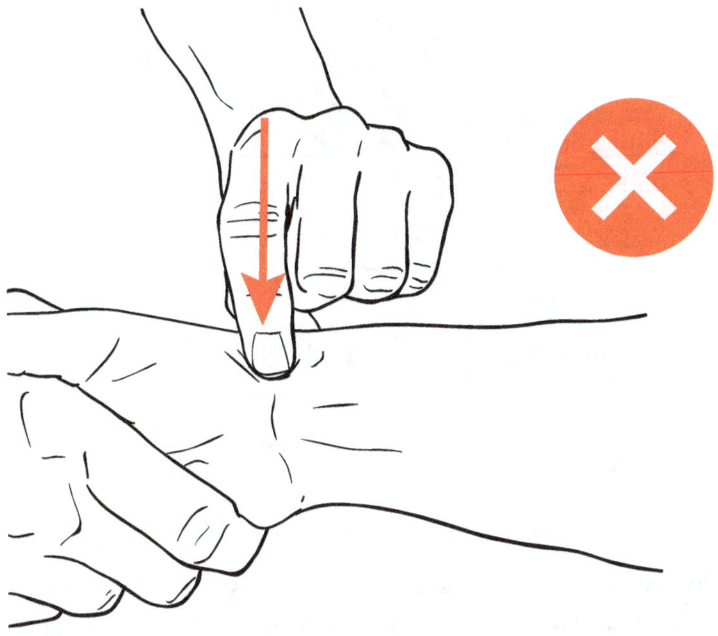

Figure 38: The index finger is not rotated

Step 9 - The Styloid Pulses And The Guan Pulse

There are three distinct pulses located in the vicinity of the styloid process on the radial artery. These three pulses are called the Distal Styloid pulse, the Apex Styloid pulse, and the Proximal Styloid pulse. They are all three located between the Cun and Guan positions. Figure 39 illustrates each of the styloid pulses. To analyze the individual pulses, first, use the index finger pad to identify the apex of the radial styloid process. This location will highlight the palpable Apex Styloid pulse. From this position palpate distally to locate the Distal Styloid pulse and proximally for the Proximal Styloid pulse. Maintain the index finger at a perpendicular angle to palpate the Apex Styloid pulse. Palpate both the DIstal Styloid and Apex Styloid pulses by rotating the index finger from the apex toward each direction.

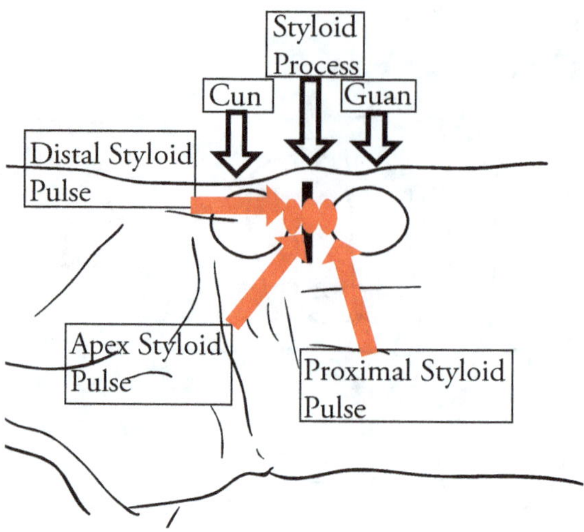

Figure 39: Distal, Proximal, and Apex Styloid Pulses

As discussed in Step 7, the styloid process serves as the partition between the Cun and Guan regions. Spreading the index finger and middle finger on either side of the styloid process is termed "gapping" the styloid and necessary for the proper location of the Guan position.

The beginner MPD practitioner can locate and palpate the Guan pulse by "gapping" the styloid (figure 40) and then substituting the middle finger with the index finger in the Guan position (figure 41). Another technique is to locate the apex styloid process pulse, on the radial artery, with the index finger and maneuver the index finger proximally past the styloid process. Upon palpation, maintain the index finger at a perpendicular angle as illustrated in figure 41.

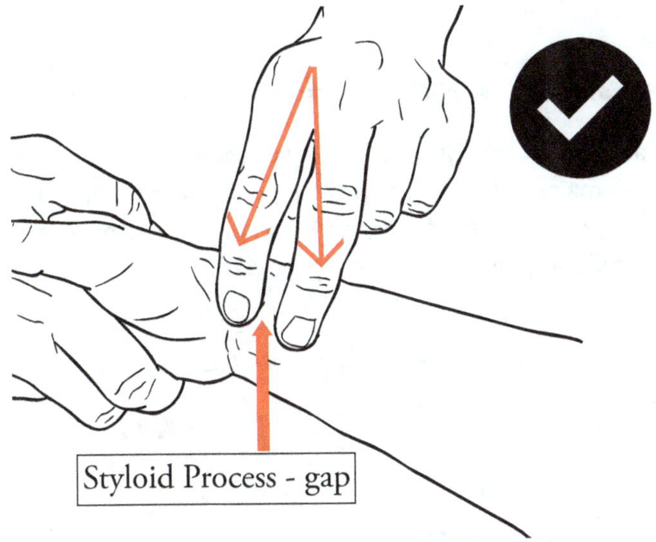

Figure 40: Gapping of the index and middle diagnostic fingers to correctly locate the Cun and Guan positions

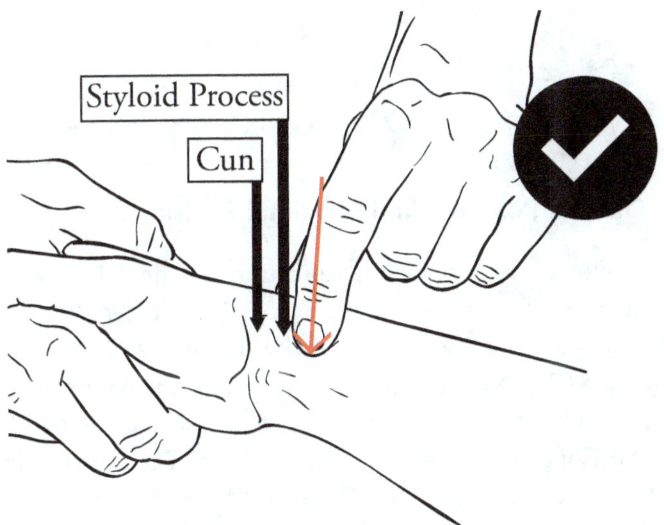

Figure 41: Guan Pulse

Step 9 - Pitfall: Tilting of Diagnostic Finger at Guan Position

In the analysis of the Guan pulse, it is necessary that the diagnostic finger pad maintains a perpendicular position. Rotating the finger distally in this position introduces the Proximal Styloid pulse and compromises the Guan pulse diagnosis (figure 42).

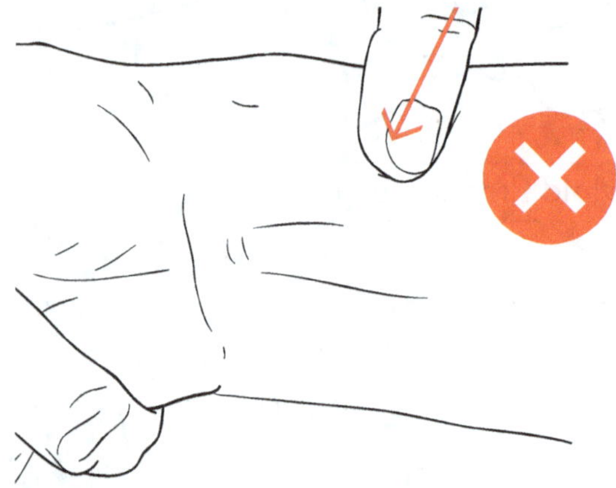

Figure 42: Incorrect rotation of index finger at Guan position

Step 10 - The Chi Position And Proximal Positions

The technique for proper identification of the Chi position is termed "The Ruler Technique." First, the diagnostic hand's index and middle fingers "gap" the styloid to identify the proper Cun and Guan positions (figure 43a). Next, both fingers are shifted proximally, which positions the index finger pad in the Guan position and the middle finger pad in the Chi position (figure 43b). The width of the styloid process, which separate the Cun and Guan positions, is also the precise distance of separation between the Guan and Chi positions. A last proximal shift of the diagnostic fingers places the index finger pad on the Chi position for optimal palpation. Maintain the diagnostic finger at a perpendicular angle to the radial artery.

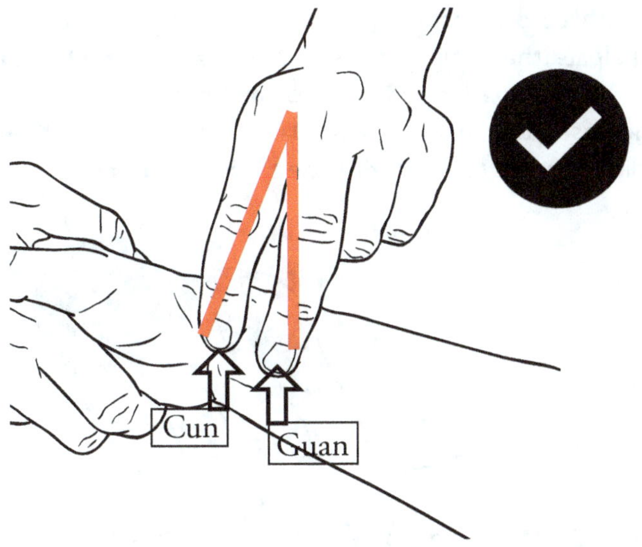

Figures 43a: Gapping the Cun and Guan positions for the Ruler Technique

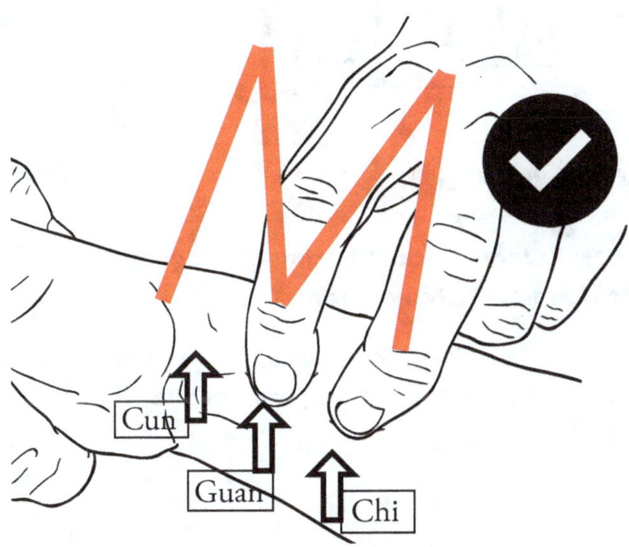

Figures 43b: The Ruler Technique for the location of Guan and Chi Positions

Figure 44 illustrates the correct placement of the diagnostic hand's index finger on the Chi position. The index, middle and ring diagnostic fingers are all touching and create a lengthened diagnostic tool, at a perpendicular angle to the radial artery, for analyzing the Proximal pulse positions. Several pathologies expressed in the Proximal pulses extend multiple finger lengths in the proximal direction of the radial

artery. The three diagnostic fingers, functioning as a unit, shift prox-imally to palpate the quality of these Proximal pulses. Use the index finger pad when palpating refined Proximal pulse presentations that require increased tactile sensitivity. Maintain the diagnostic fingers at a perpendicular angle for analyzing the Proximal pulses.

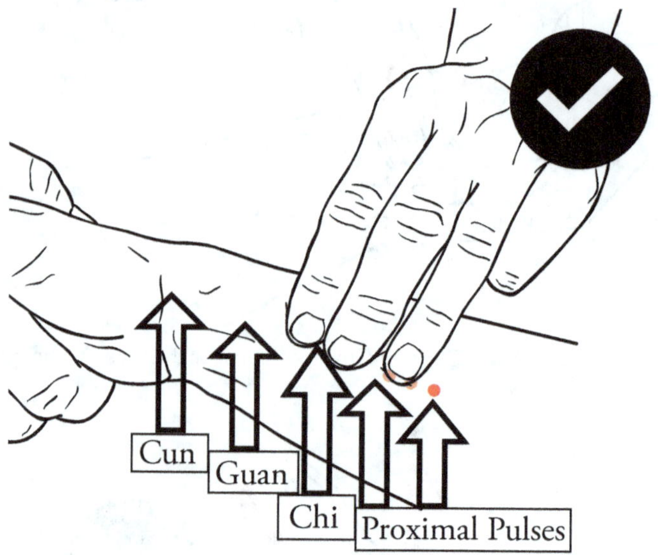

Figure 44: Correct location of the Chi and Proximal Pulse positions

Step 10 - Pitfall: Inadequate Spacing Of Fingers At Guan And Chi Positions

Figure 45 illustrates incorrect spacing between the Guan and Chi positions compromising proper diagnosis of the Chi and potential Proximal pulses.

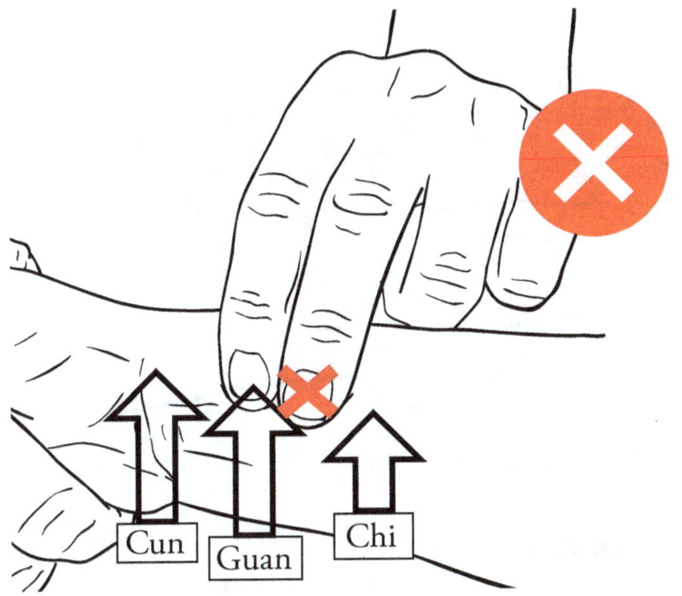

Figure 45: Neglecting to use the "Ruler Technique" distorts proper analysis of the Chi and the Proximal Pulses

The Cun, Styloid, Guan and Chi Pulses represent physiological pulses that always display a healthy (physiological) or aberrated (pathological) pulse condition. The Yin Wei, Yang Wei, Large Vessel, Mitral Valve and the Proximal pulses also display a healthy or aberrated pulse condition.

The Cun, Styloid, Guan and Chi positions all have a central section enclosed by a proximal, distal, medial and lateral section. Each part can highlight distinct anatomical and physiological information. With experience, the MPD practitioner develops the refined sensitivity to distinguish these different sections for enhanced diagnostic precision.

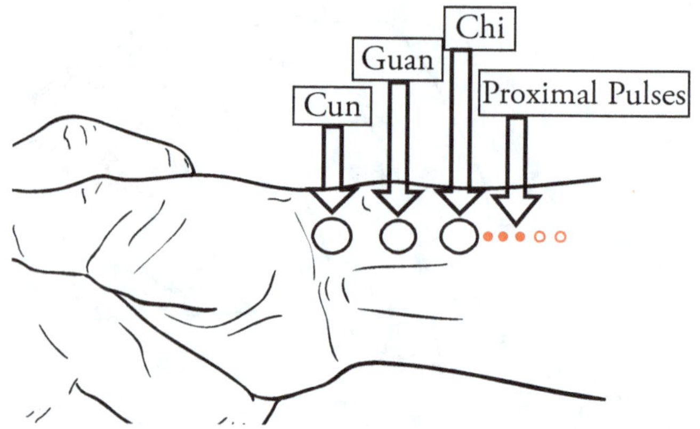

Figure 46: Location of the Cun, Guan, Chi and Proximal Pulse positions

Step 11 - Brachial Pulse

Steps 1-10 are the essential instructions for proper MPD diagnostic positioning on the radial artery. Steps 11-12 are additional procedures focused on palpation of the elbow region to highlight relevant diagnostic information. After palpating the pulses at the wrist, palpate the Brachial pulse at the elbow region. This pulse is essential for correct diagnosis in patients with severe vascular-compromised conditions that distort arterial blood circulation in the lower arm.

Start this process by gently flexing and stabilizing the patient's elbow. Use the index and middle fingers of the opposite hand to palpate the brachial pulse, located medial to the biceps brachii tendon at the antecubital crease. This pulse is also palpable in the slightly proximal direction, between the bicep and the brachialis muscle (figure 47 and 48).

There are situations in which the patient's radial pulses display a systemically weak or blocked presentation, yet the Brachial pulse is strongly palpable (e.g., systemic inflammation). In these cases, the blood circulation is obstructed in the lower arm, and the diagnostic analysis should be relevant to the Brachial pulse presentation. It is incorrect to treat these patients with a tonifying herbal strategy based on the compromised radial pulse analysis.

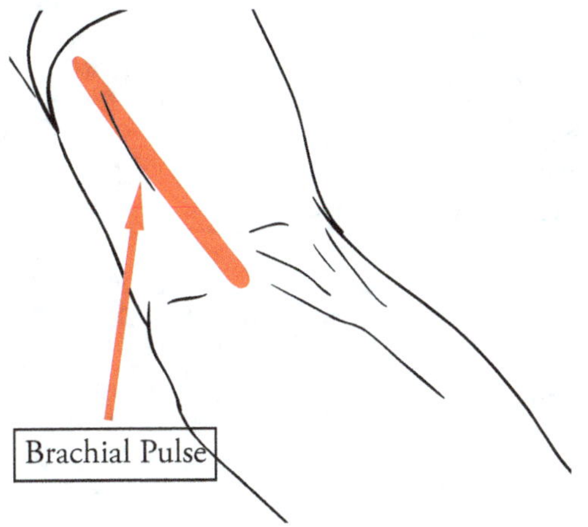

Figure 47: Brachial Pulse

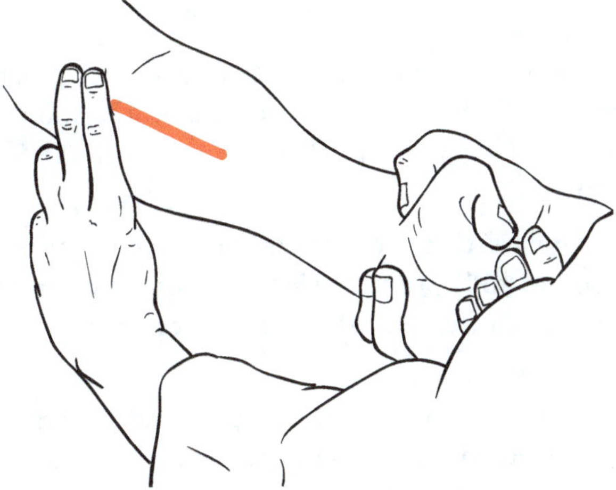

Figure 48: Palpation of Brachial Pulse

Step 12 - Temperature Lateral Elbow

The final diagnostic step involves using the dorsal side of the diagnosing hand to palpate the general skin temperature of the patient's lateral elbow region. Palpate the skin temperature above the brachioradialis muscle at the level of the elbow crease. This region is in between the acupuncture points LI (Large Intestine) 11 and 10, as shown in figure 49.

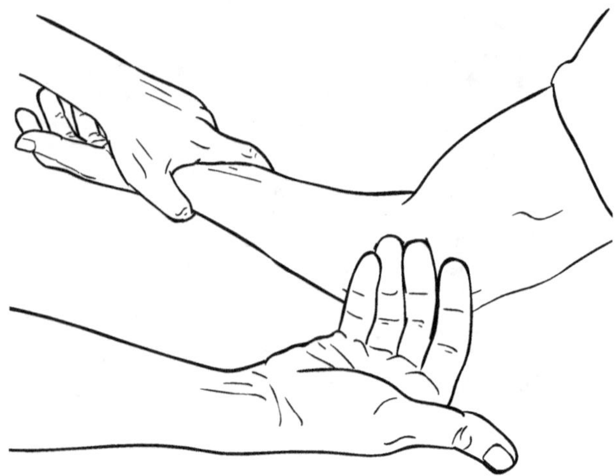

Figure 49: Taking the temperature of the lateral elbow crease region

(Lateral view on radial aspect of elbow and forearm)

The palpation of a cool/cold skin temperature highlights a weak digestive function. In these cases, the addition of formulas to bolster digestion, such as Ping Wei San (平胃散) or An Zhong San (安中散) are appropriate.

Instruct patients that are wearing long-sleeve shirts to lift the sleeves before the MPD process. This provides sufficient time for the lateral elbow temperature to adjust for the correct temperature assessment.

While uncommon, some patients have a radial artery that is anatomically displaced. In these cases, the radial artery deviates to the dorsal/posterior side of the wrist as opposed to the standard ventral/anterior position. This issue often presents only on one side, and proper diagnosis ensues by analyzing the normal side pulse and the brachial pulse.

Ten Common Mistakes And How To Avoid Them

1. Ensure proper palpation of the five Cun position-related pulses (Cun pulse, Yin Wei pulse, Yang Wei pulse, Large Vessel pulse and Mitral Valve pulse). Note that the Yin Wei pulse and Large Vessel pulse are assessed only on the left side.

2. Upon analyzing the Cun pulse, rotate the diagnostic hand's index finger pad 30-40 degrees distally, toward the scaphoid bone. The diagnostic index finger is rotated slightly for the Distal and Proximal Styloid pulses. Do not rotate the diagnostic fingers for the Apex Styloid, Guan, Chi and Proximal pulses.

3. The Large Vessel pulse is precisely located at the wrist crease junction of the superficial palmar arch, the flexor carpi radialis tendon, and the scaphoid bone. Compressed pen-tip pulses palpated distal or medial to this junction are not considered the Large Vessel pulse.

4. Do not confuse the Yin Wei pulse or Yang Wei pulse for the Cun pulse. Palpate the Cun pulse with the rotated finger pad in the central region of the Cun "valley." Palpate the Large Vessel pulse with a slight rotation and the other Cun "valley" pulses with the finger pad at the perpendicular angle.

5. Properly "gap" the radial styloid process to locate the Cun and Guan positions. With palpating the Guan position, ensure that the diagnostic finger pad is not on the Proximal Styloid pulse.

6. Following the proper "gapping" of the radial styloid process, use the "Ruler Technique" to correctly identify the Chi position. The Proximal pulses are located immediately proximal to the Chi position and can extend several finger lengths in the proximal direction.

7. Improper positioning of the finger pads too medially, adjacent to the flexor carpi radialis tendon, compromises correct pulse diagnosis.

8. Palpate the pulses predominantly using the diagnostic hand's index finger pad. Include the other finger pads in the palpation of the Proximal pulses or testing for systemic pulses described in Chapter 7. Do not palpate the pulses with an excessive pressure that occludes the radial artery.

9. Palpate the Brachial pulse in the presence of systemic weak or blocked pulses. If the Brachial pulse is of forceful quality, do not diagnose based on the compromised radial artery circulation.

10. Palpate the general skin temperature at the radial/lateral region of the elbow crease. This temperature highlights the general function of the patient's digestive system.

4

Pulse Positions - Anatomical Correspondences and Conditions

Each specific pulse position corresponds to distinct biophysical organ systems and anatomical regions of the body. The MPD analysis can present the structural and functional states of these particular anatomical components.

A most innovative discovery of Chinese Medicine is the highly integrated view of the body, involving the internal organ systems, the neuro-vascular systems, and the external musculoskeletal system. These biophysical connections generate the expression of the visceral-somatic (organ-body), somato-visceral (body-organ), somato-somatic (body-body) and visceral-visceral (organ-organ) expressions of the body. In the practice of Chinese Medicine, the recognition of these integrated mechanisms concerning disease directs the proper therapeutic actions.

The MPD analysis of specific pulse positions clarifies the physical condition of the organ systems and anatomical regions. The comprehensive pulse analysis informs the practitioner of the multiple pathological conditions influencing each patient's disease patterns. This comprehensive diagnosis guides the most effective MPD treatment strategies.

The ensuing text describes the anatomical correspondences and conditions of each pulse position in detail. The beginner MPD practitioner must memorize these specific anatomical correspondences to diagnose patient conditions efficiently.

Figure 50 illustrates all of the MPD pulse positions of the right arm. The left arm pulse positions are identical to the right, with the inclusion of the mitral valve pulse.

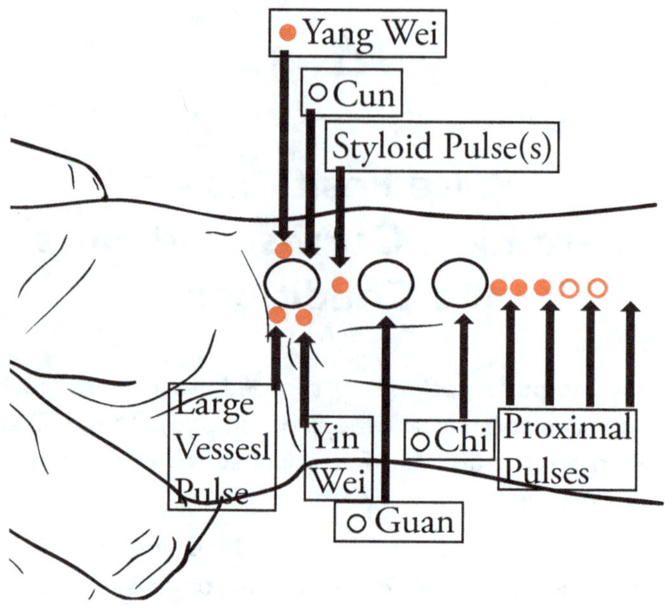

Figure 50: Locations of Cun, Guan, Chi, Yang Wei, Yin Wei,
Large Vessel, Styloid and Proximal Pulses

Right Arm

Right Cun Pulse

The right Cun pulse position (figure 51) informs on the condition of the head region, with a particular focus on the paranasal sinuses of the upper respiratory tract. Specific pulse presentations also highlight the vascular state of the head/brain region and can reveal previous head injuries and the expression of vertigo, inner ear, and eye conditions. This position also provides an assessment of the general health of the immune system, allergic responses to air-borne allergies, flu and acute colds.

The right Cun also informs on the condition of the Large Intestine. This position can reflect peristalsis function, polyps, hemorrhoids and symptoms associated with Diverticulitis, Diverticulosis and Irritable bowel syndrome (IBS).

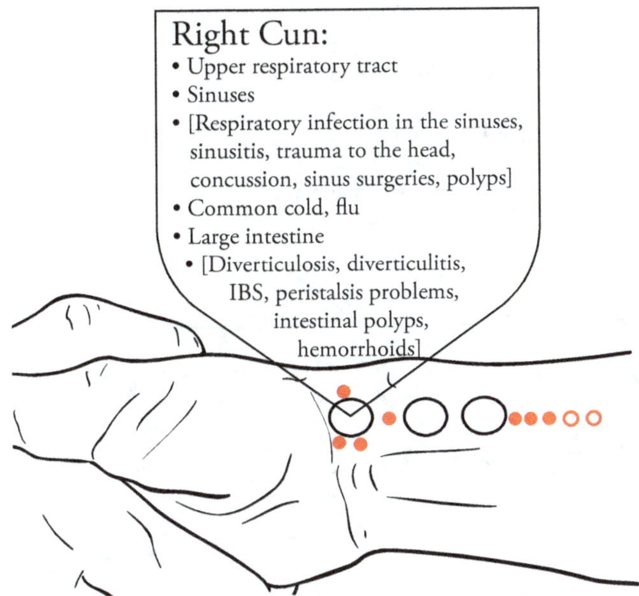

Figure 51: Right Cun pulse position and its correspondence to the upper respiratory tract, the large intestine, and associated conditions

Right Yang Wei Pulse

The right Yang Wei pulse position (figure 52) informs on conditions of the lower respiratory tract. The most common conditions represented are asthma, bronchitis, COPD, general respiratory inflammation and acute colds.

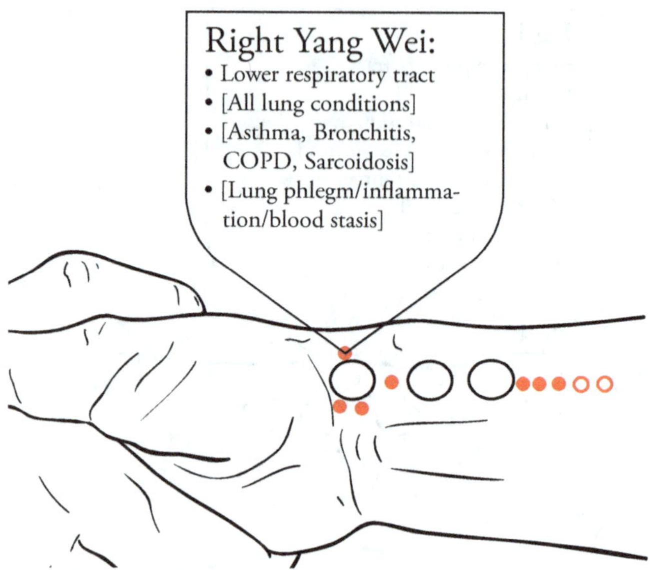

Figure 52: Right Yang Wei pulse position and its correspondence to the lower respiratory tract and associated conditions

Right Styloid Pulses

The pulses of the right radial styloid region correspond with the anatomy of the throat (pharynx, larynx, trachea, thyroid, and esophagus). The most common clinical diagnoses are as follows: The Distal Styloid pulse represents the superior throat region and the common symptom of post-nasal drip. The Apex Styloid pulse can diagnose thyroid gland conditions and pharyngitis. The Proximal Styloid pulse can diagnose gastric reflux and esophageal hernias.

Figure 53 illustrates the anatomical correspondences and conditions of the right Styloid positions. Figure 54 illustrates the location of the three Styloid pulses.

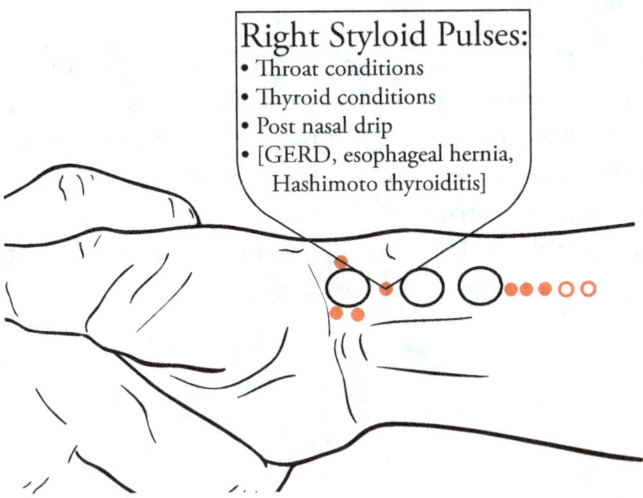

Figure 53: Right Styloid pulses and its correspondence to throat diseases, e.g., thyroid gland diseases, post-nasal drip, esophageal hernia and gastric reflux

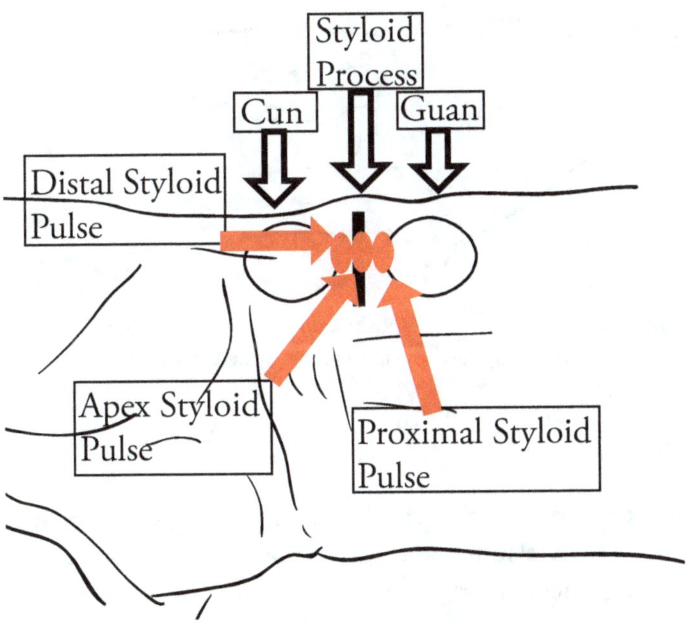

Figure 54: Location of the Distal, Apex and Proximal Styloid pulse positions

Right Guan Pulse

The right Guan pulse position (figure 55) corresponds to the stomach and pancreas organs. This region informs of the functional state of the digestive system and particular gastrointestinal conditions. Specific pulse presentations relate to common western medical conditions, such as gastritis, H. Pylori, and gastric ulcers. In combination, specific right and left Guan pulse presentations can represent the development of Type 2 diabetes and insulin resistance.

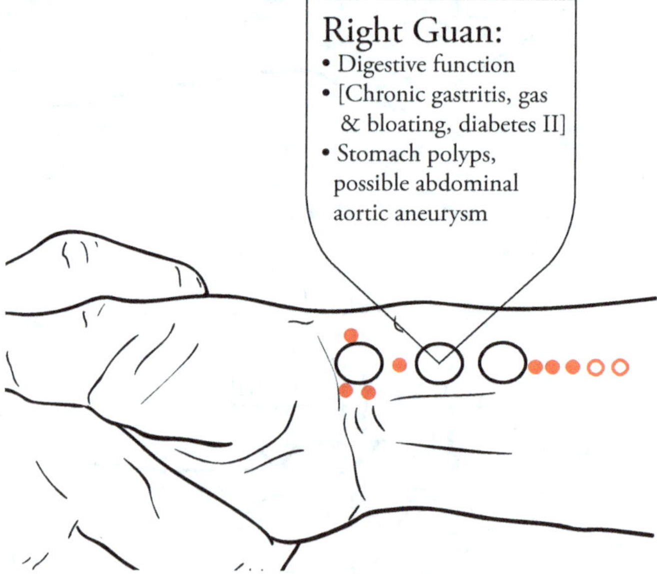

Figure 55: Right Guan pulse position and its correspondence to gastrointestinal conditions related to the stomach and pancreas

Right Chi Pulse

The right Chi pulse position (figure 56) corresponds to the function of the kidneys, bladder, and the urinary system. Kidney disease, kidney stones (specific to right ureter), urinary tract infections (UTI) and urinary incontinence are common clinical conditions presented in the right Chi. The combination of particular right and left Chi pulses represent prostate issues.

This position also corresponds to the upper thoracic region and shoulder girdle, with emphasis on the rotator cuff complex. Potential conditions are frozen shoulder, shoulder tissue damage, thoracic muscular tension, thoracic osteophytes and vertebral damage.

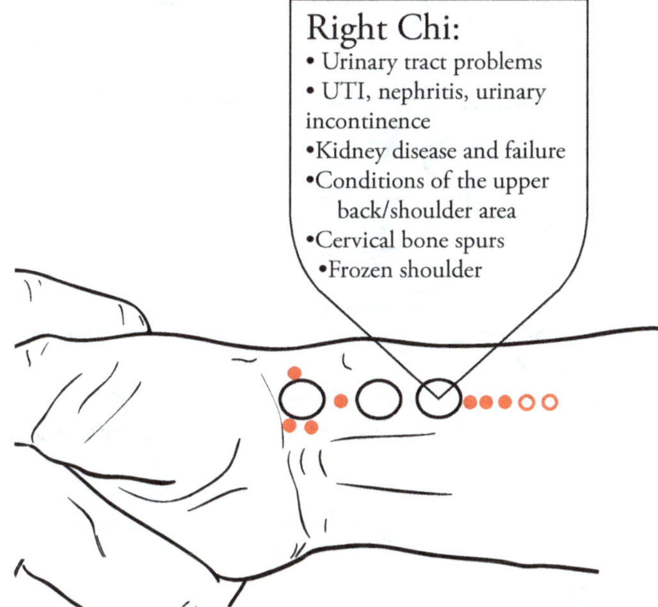

Figure 56: Right Chi pulse position and its correspondence to the kidneys, urinary system, thoracic and shoulder regions

Right Proximal Pulses

The right Proximal pulse position (figure 57) informs on the functional state of the upper thoracic/cervical region. Clinically, specific right Proximal pulses reflect neck pain and related issues, such as sprains/strains, cervical osteophytes, herniated discs, compressed spinal nerves, chronic headaches and migraines.

When detected with specific right Chi pulses, the right Proximal pulses represent conditions of the urinary system. Also, a superficial and pounding pulse presentation on both sides indicates low-level chemical poisoning or multiple chemical sensitivities.

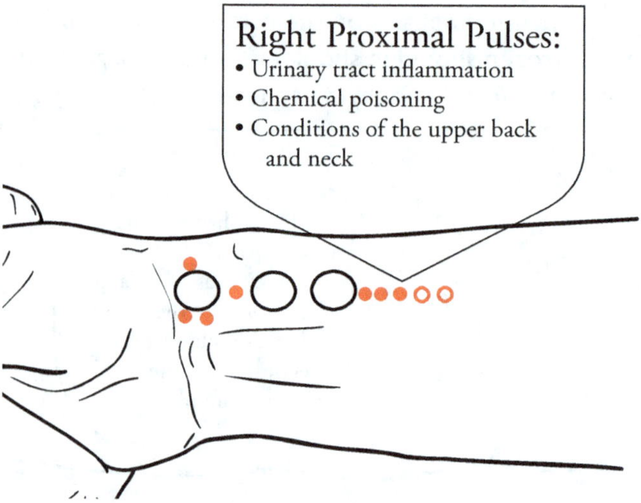

Figure 57: Right Proximal pulse position and its correspondence to the upper thoracic/cervical region, urinary system, and potential chemical poisoning

Left Arm

Left Cun

All of the left Cun "valley" pulses, except the left Yang Wei pulse, correspond to the cardiac region and inform on conditions of the heart and pericardium. Specific pulse presentations of the left Cun also reflect small intestine conditions. The Yin Wei, Large Vessel and Mitral Valve pulses, all associated with cardiac conditions, are only assessed on the left side. Clinical experience has demonstrated these same pulses are inconclusive diagnostic tools on the right side. The only exception could be the palpation of a mitral valve pulse on the right side. The presence of this pulse may be indicative of a valve problem, either between the right atrium and ventricle or the pulmonary valve. More research is needed in this case.

The left Cun "valley" pulses, related to cardiac health, are essential in clinical practice. According to the American Heart Association and the American Stroke Association's Heart Disease and Stroke Statistics 2017, cardiovascular disease is the leading cause of death in the United States. Cardiovascular disease accounted for 31% of global deaths in 2013, with that number estimated to increase drastically by 2030. In the United States, cardiovascular disease kills more people each year than all forms of cancer and chronic lower respiratory conditions combined. Published in 2016, a follow-up study of the Framingham Heart Study (currently analyzing 3rd generation participants) diagnosed nearly 60% of participants (average age 51) with preclinical heart failure.

The prevalence of preclinical heart disease has been convincingly validated over twenty years of clinical experience seeing more than 500,000 patient visits. The refinements of the left Cun pulses and their related cardiac conditions have developed alongside detailed patient medical histories and recurrent confirmation with cardiac diagnostic testing. MPD can reveal the specific suboptimal function of the cardiac system and can thereby direct corrective and prophylactic herbal therapies.

The left Cun pulse position (figure 58) can inform on cardiac conditions, such as preclinical heart failure, coronary artery disease, coronary arterial spasms or angina pectoris. This position also highlights the common patient symptoms of chronic fatigue, insomnia, and anxiety. Clinical experience has shown that these common clinical symptoms relate to various dysfunctions of the heart and vascular system.

The left Cun pulse position can reveal conditions of the small intestine such as Chrohn's disease, Ulcerative colitis, enteritis and the symptoms of gas and bloating, if the causative factor is a dysfunctional small intestine.

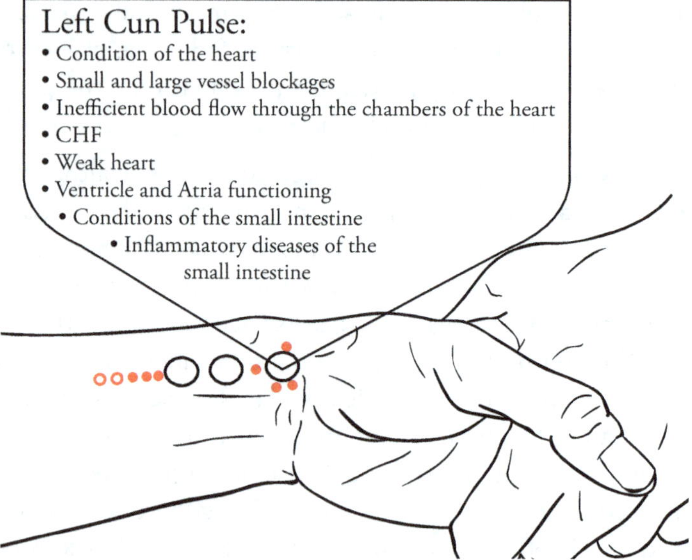

Figure 58: Left Cun pulse position and its correspondence to the condition of the heart, pericardium and small intestine

Figure **59** and **60** detail the anatomical regions of the left Cun pulse position. With experience, MPD provides refined diagnostic information regarding the functional condition of the specific regions of the heart.

Figure **59** illustrates the medial (ulnar) and lateral (radial) regions of the left Cun position. The medial aspect corresponds to the right-sided coronary vasculature, and the lateral aspect corresponds to the left-sided coronary vasculature.

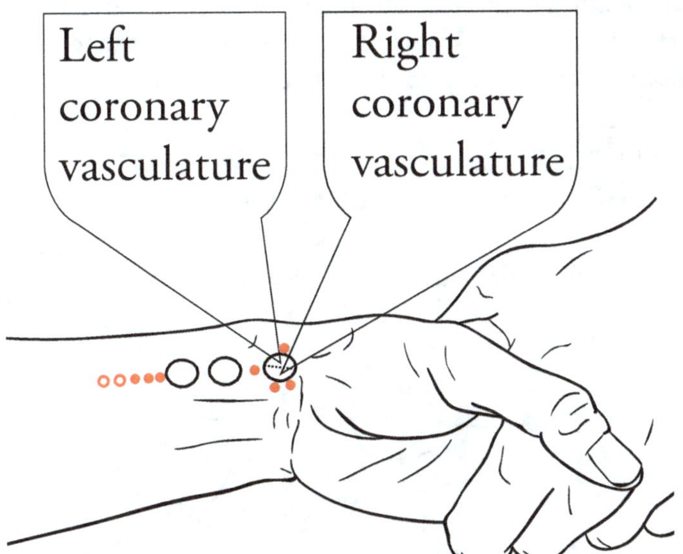

Figure 59: Left Cun pulse position and the location of the left and the right side coronary vasculature

Figure 60 illustrates the distal and proximal regions of the left Cun pulse position. The proximal aspect corresponds to the coronary vasculature and function of the ventricular chambers. The distal aspect corresponds to the coronary vasculature and function of the atrial chambers. The differential diagnosis of western medical heart conditions often relates to specific structural and functional compensations of these heart regions. The proximal and distal Cun regions facilitate the comparison of atrial vs. ventricular size, strength and vascular health, which relate to many western medical heart conditions. Heart insufficiency, various cardiomyopathies, and mitral valve regurgitations correspond to these left Cun regions.

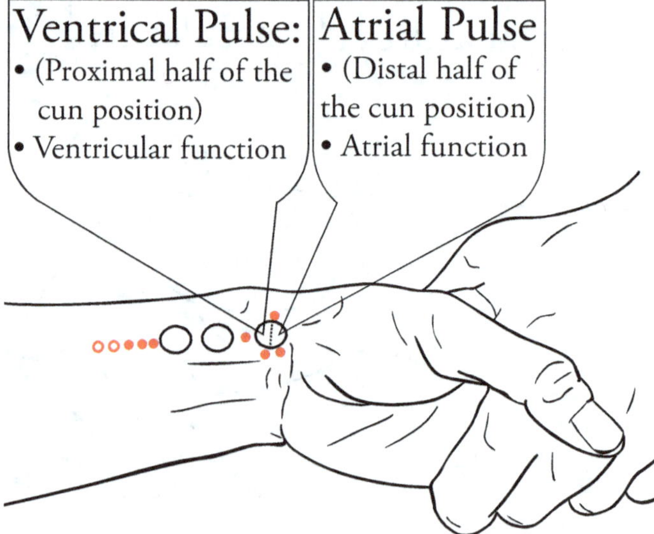

Figure 60: Left Cun pulse position and location of the atrial and ventricular regions

Yin Wei Pulse

In the MPD system, the Yin Wei pulse position (figure 61) is analyzed only on the left arm. The presence of a palpable pulse in the Yin Wei position can be indicative of heart-related symptoms, such as shortness of breath, palpitations, angina pectoris and potentially high levels of low-density lipoprotein (LDL) cholesterol. The presence of this pulse can be an indication of hereditary heart disease or genetic risk factors for the development of heart disease.

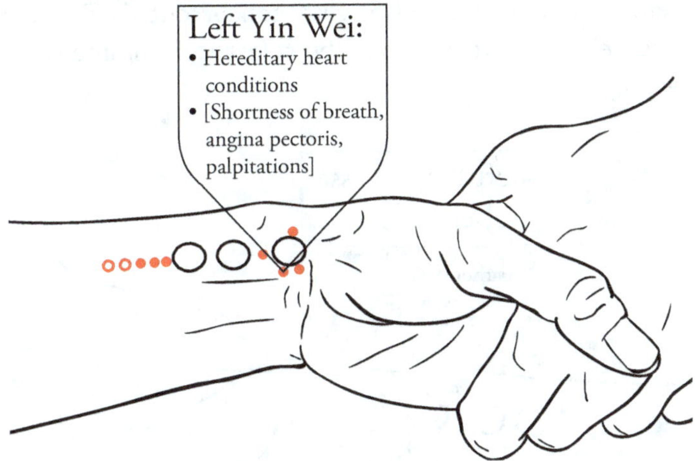

Figure 61: Left Yin Wei Pulse and its correspondence to hereditary heart conditions and heart symptoms

Large Vessel Pulse

When palpable, the Large Vessel pulse (figure 62) can represent a restriction of blood circulation to the large coronary arteries. This pulse is evident as a defined compressed like pulse (feels like the tip of a ballpoint pen). Increased hardness and strength of this pulse represents a worsened circulatory condition in the large coronary arteries, usually due to vessel damage, narrowing or spasm. The Large Vessel pulse is commonly palpable in combination with both the pathological left Cun and Yin Wei pulses. A patient with a forceful, unmistakable Large Vessel pulse, with concurrent CAD (Coronary artery disease) risk factors, should be referred for immediate cardiologic testing.

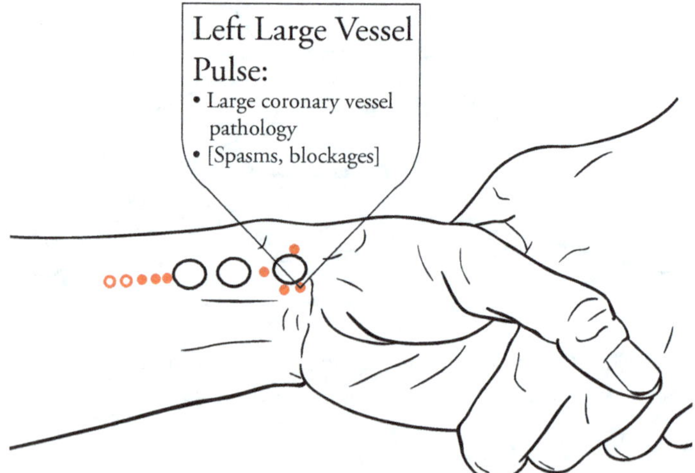

Figure 62: Left Large Vessel Pulse and its correspondence to large coronary vessel pathology

Mitral Valve Pulse

The palpation of a markedly noticeable Mitral Valve pulse (figure 63) represents general heart valve conditions, most commonly mitral valve related. The heart valves maintain efficient unidirectional blood circulation within the heart. Weakness or rigidity of the valves may lead to regurgitation of blood within the heart and the compromised functioning of specific heart chambers. The pathological left Mitral Valve pulse is commonly palpable with particular pulses of the atrial and ventricular regions of the left Cun.

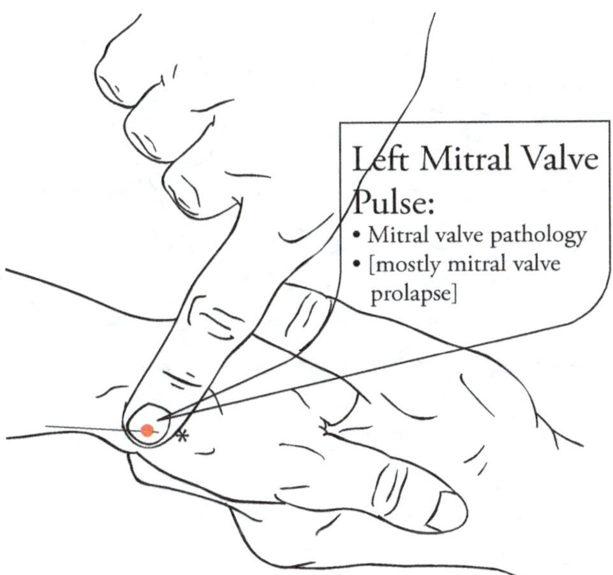

Figure 63: Left Mitral Valve Pulse and its correspondence to heart valve conditions (most commonly mitral valve dysfunction)

(*Abductor pollicis longus tendon)

Left Yang Wei Pulse

The left Yang Wei pulse position (figure 64) informs on the systemic conditions of the joints and connective tissues. The presence of various pulse qualities distinguish conditions such as osteoarthritis, rheumatoid arthritis, and other rheumatoid disorders.

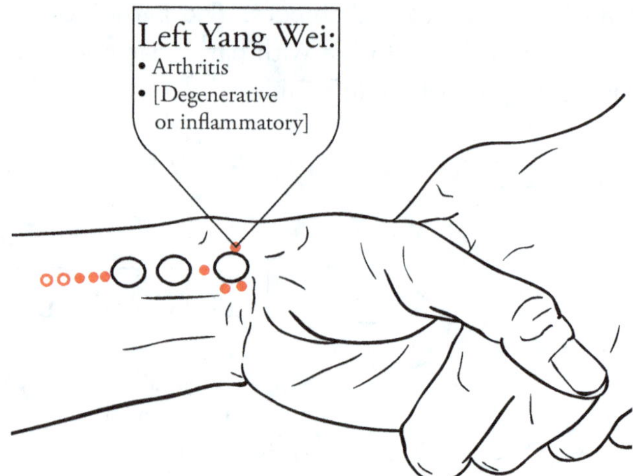

Figure 64: Left Yang Wei pulse postion and its correspondence to arthritis and other rheumatoid disorders

Left Styloid Pulses

The left side and right side Styloid pulse poitions correspond to different anatomical regions. The left radial styloid pulse position (figure 65) corresponds to the diaphragm region and associated conditions. The most common clinical diagnoses are as follows: In combination with the left Cun ventricular portion, the left Distal Styloid pulse can inform on the function of the left ventricle. The Apex Styloid pulse can diagnose diaphragmatic issues and hiatal hernias. The Proximal Styloid pulse can diagnose gastric reflux and potential upper liver enlargement.

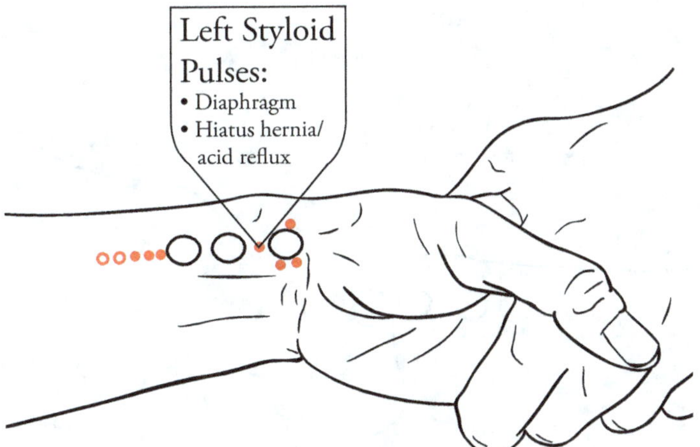

Figure 65: Left Styloid pulse postion and its correspondence to the diaphragm, gastric reflux, hiatal hernia

Left Guan Pulse

The left Guan pulse position (figure 66) corresponds to the liver and gallbladder organ systems. Hepatic and biliary conditions, such as fatty liver disease, hepatic cysts, hepatic artery aneurysms and gall-stones can represent in the left Guan position.

Two thousand years of Chinese Medicine empirical evidence has demonstrated an intimate correlation between these organ systems and the expression of mental/emotional states. The left Guan position informs on symptoms of irritability, frustration, depression and apathy.

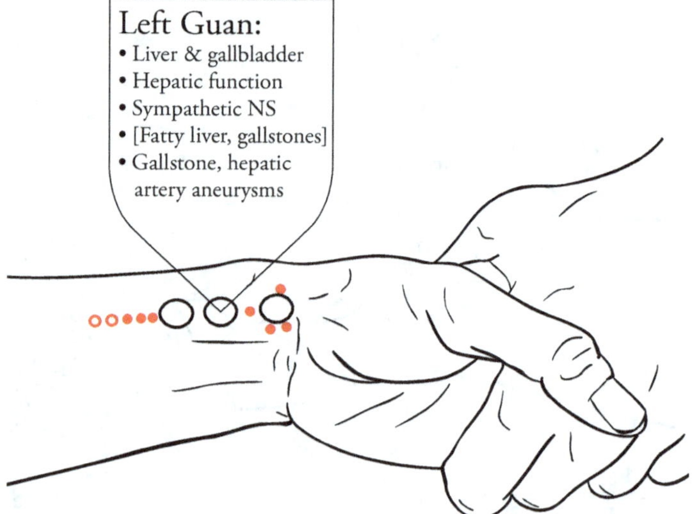

Figure 66: Left Guan pulse position and its correspondence to liver and gallbladder conditions and mental/emotional conditions

Left Chi Pulse

The left Chi pulse position (figure 67) corresponds to the function of the reproductive and endocrine systems (primarily adrenal function). Specific pulses can indicate infertility, low libido, impotence and adrenal fatigue syndrome. This pulse position can reflect the presence of kidney stones particular to the left ureter. In women, specific pulses can indicate a history of lower abdominal surgeries, abortions, and partial/full hysterectomies. In men, the combination of particular left and right Chi pulses represent prostate issues.

This position also corresponds to the physical condition of the hip, knee and ankle regions. The distal aspect of the left Chi pulse position represents the hip region. The central aspect represents the knee region, and the proximal aspect represents the ankle region. Particular pulse presentations differentiate acute and chronic tissue damage, tendonitis, bursitis, rheumatoid and osteoarthritis.

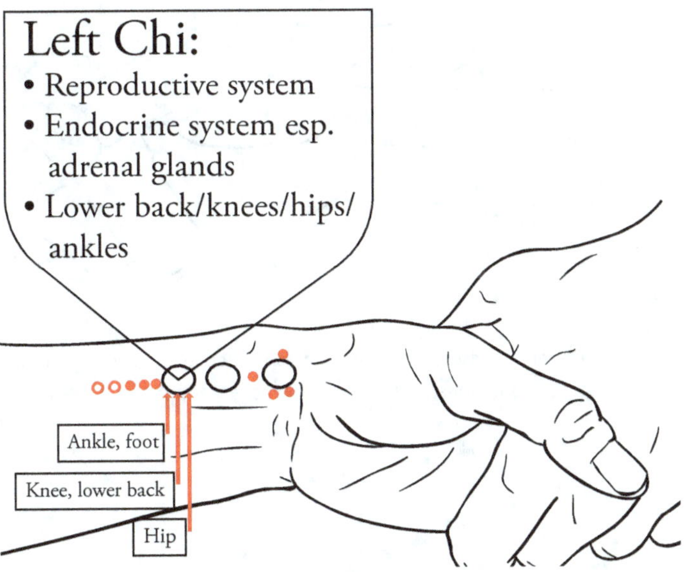

Figure 67: Left Chi pulse position and its correspondence to the reproductive system, endocrine system (e.g., adrenal glands), knee, hip and ankle regions

Left Proximal Pulses

The left Proximal pulse position (figure **68**) informs on the functional condition of the lumbar region. Clinically, specific left Proximal pulses reflect lumbar region pain and related issues, such as sprains/strains, spinal osteophytes, herniated discs, compressed spinal nerves and paresthesia conditions.

Specific left Proximal pulses also represent uterine and ovarian conditions, such as endometriosis, uterine fibroids and PCOS (polycystic ovarian syndrome).

A superficial and pounding proximal pulse on both sides indicates low-level chemical poisoning or multiple chemical sensitivities.

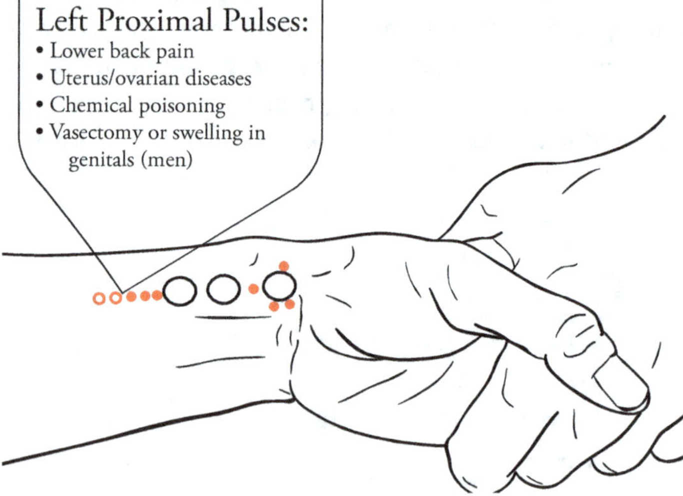

Figure 68: Left Proximal pulse position its correspondence to conditions of the lumbar region, uterus/ovarian conditions, chemical poisoning, vasectomy or prostate enlargement

Conclusion

MPD proficiency in the clinic is dependent on a systematic course of action. The 12 steps for proper positioning are the foundation for the correct MPD diagnosis. It is the integration of proper positioning and the knowledge of each pulse position's anatomical correspondences/conditions that instruct the precise diagnosis. With clinical experience, these operations become embedded to memory and are executed as second nature.

5

Assessment of the Physiological (Healthy) Pulse Depth

The Cun, Guan, and Chi pulses each have a distinct physiological depth that represents the healthy function of the corresponding organ systems and anatomical regions.

These distinct pulse depth and quality descriptions are unique to MPD and serve as the foundation for diagnosis and treatment strategies. The MPD treatment objective is to identify the specific pulse aberrations, reflecting particular health conditions, and reestablish the healthy physiological pulses.

Figure 69 illustrates the five levels of the pulse depth.

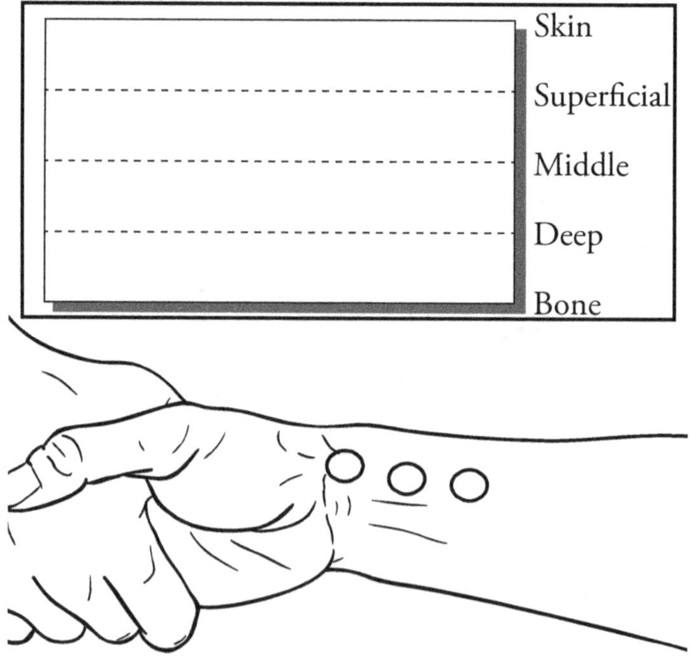

Figure 69: Five levels of pulse depths

Skin Level:

Palpate the skin level by placing the diagnostic hand's finger pads on the skin above the pulse positions. No pressure is applied to perceive the pulse at this level. The skin level is a pathological pulse depth that invariably represents dysfunction of the corresponding organ systems/anatomical regions of the pulse positions.

Superficial Level:

Palpate the superficial level with gentle pressure just below the skin level. This depth is the proper physiological depth of both the right and left Cun positions.

Middle Level:

Palpate the middle level with gentle pressure below the superficial level. This depth is the proper physiological depth of both the right and left Guan positions.

Deep Level:

Palpate the deep level with gentle pressure below the middle level. This depth is the proper physiological depth of both the right and left Chi positions.

Bone Level:

Palpate the bone level with sufficient pressure to the level just above the radial bone. The bone level is a pathological pulse depth that invariably represents dysfunction of the corresponding organ systems/anatomical regions of the pulse positions.

An additional technique for assessing the specific pulse depths involves locating the skin level, bone level, and middle level. First, identify the skin level by placing the diagnostic hand's finger pads on the skin without applying pressure. Next, identify the bone level by applying substantial pressure to the level just above the bone. Then, locate the middle level in between the skin and bone levels. The proper identification of these three levels provides a reference point for the location of all five depth levels.

It is common to palpate the pulse at multiple levels within a single position. The depth in which the pulse is most discernible is considered the "pulse center." For example, the patient's right Guan pulse is palpable at the middle level, but more obvious and forceful at the deep level. In this case, the right Guan "pulse center" is considered the deep level, which represents a pathological pulse and corresponding health condition.

Physiological (Healthy) Pulse Depths

The physiological depth of each pulse position is commonly referred to as the "proper home." This is the MPD benchmark for identifying the healthy pulse and healthy condition of each corresponding organ system and anatomical region. The foundational step of MPD diagnosis is to identify the pulses that deviate from the "proper home" (physiological depth) and require therapeutic resolution. Figures 70-75 show the physiological pulse depths of all three principal positions (Cun, Guan, Chi).

The Right And Left Cun Pulses

The physiological pulse, of the right and left Cun position, is a slightly convex pulse at the superficial level. The strongest quality is palpable at the superficial level and decreases at the middle and deep levels. The physiological pulse is not evident in either the skin or bone levels. Figure 70 illustrates the physiological depth and convex quality of the Cun pulse.

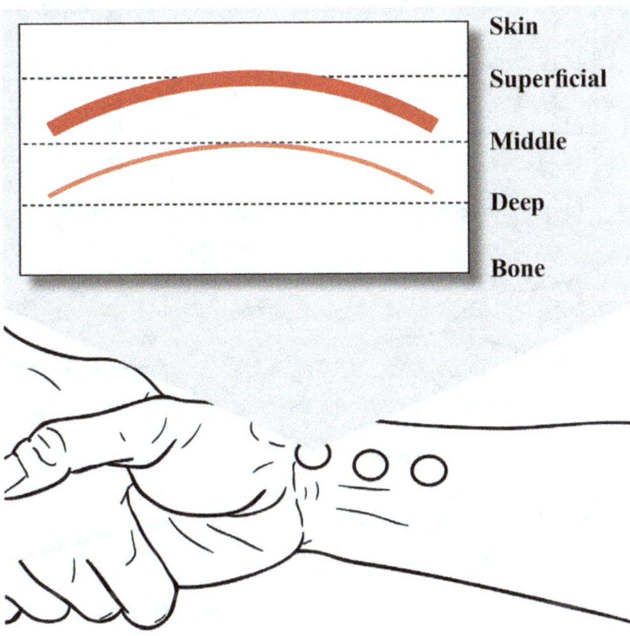

Figure 70: Right and left Cun physiological depths

The Right Guan Pulse

The physiological pulse of the right Guan is as a slightly convex pulse at the middle level. This healthy pulse is not palpable above or below the middle level. Figure 71 illustrates the physiological depth and convex quality of the right Guan pulse.

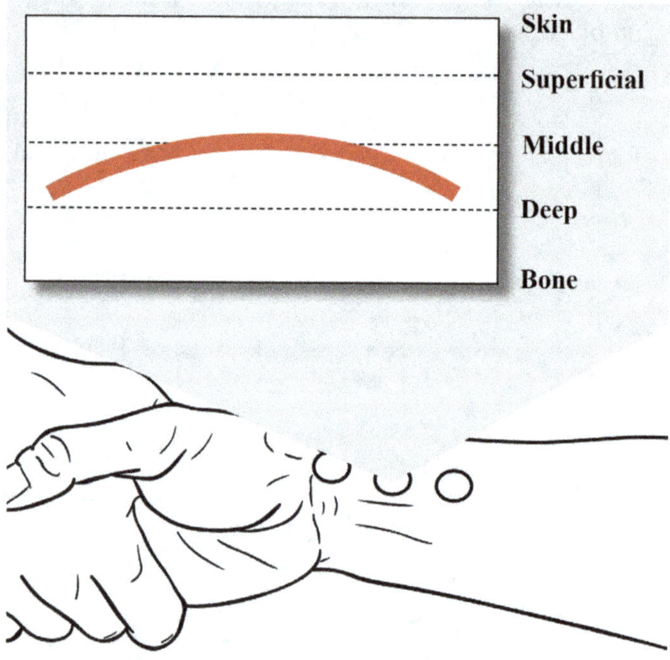

Figure 71: Right Guan physiological depth

The Left Guan Pulse

The physiological pulse of the left Guan is a slightly wiry pulse at the middle level. This healthy pulse is not palpable above or below the middle level. Figure 72 illustrates the physiological depth and wiry quality of the left Guan pulse.

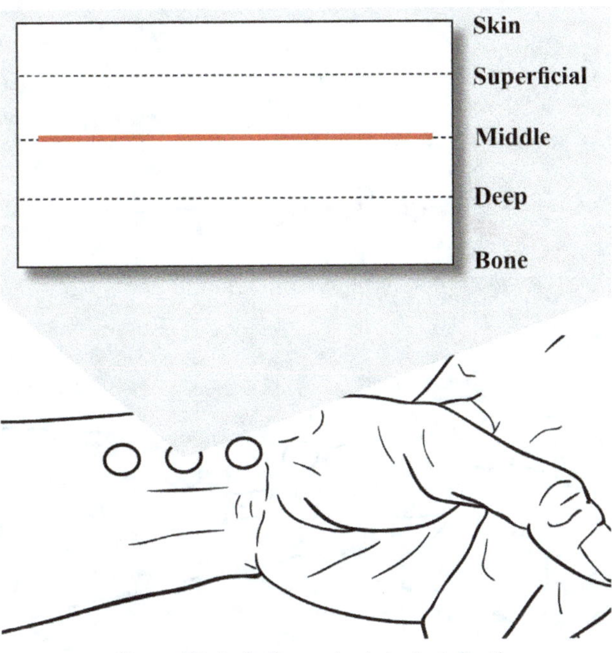

Figure 72: Left Guan physiological depth

The Right And Left Chi Pulses

The physiological pulse of the right and left Chi position is a slightly convex pulse at the deep level. This healthy pulse is not palpable above the deep level. Figure 73 illustrates the physiological depth and convex quality of the Chi pulse.

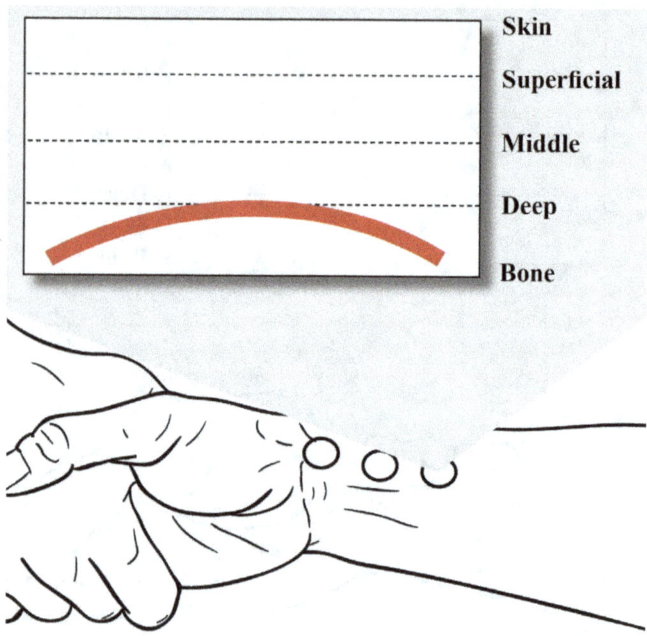

Figure 73: Right and Left Chi physiological depths

Figure 74 illustrates the healthy pulse presentation of the Cun, Guan and Chi pulse positions. Note that the overall healthy pulse presents in a descending manner, from the Cun to Chi positions. This descending pulse presentation relates to the anatomical positioning of the radial artery. The wrist crease is the most shallow position of the radial artery. In the proximal direction, toward the elbow, the artery positions at deeper levels amidst the tissues of the forearm.

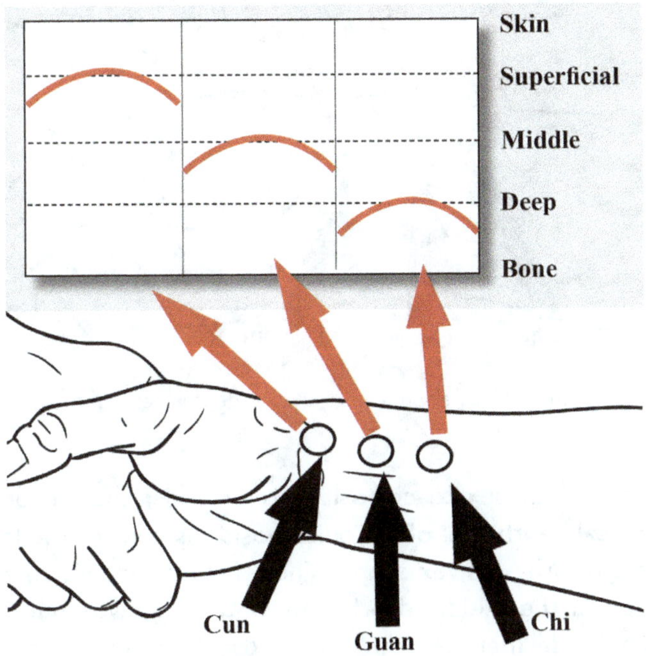

Figure 74: Proper physiological pulse depths (right hand)

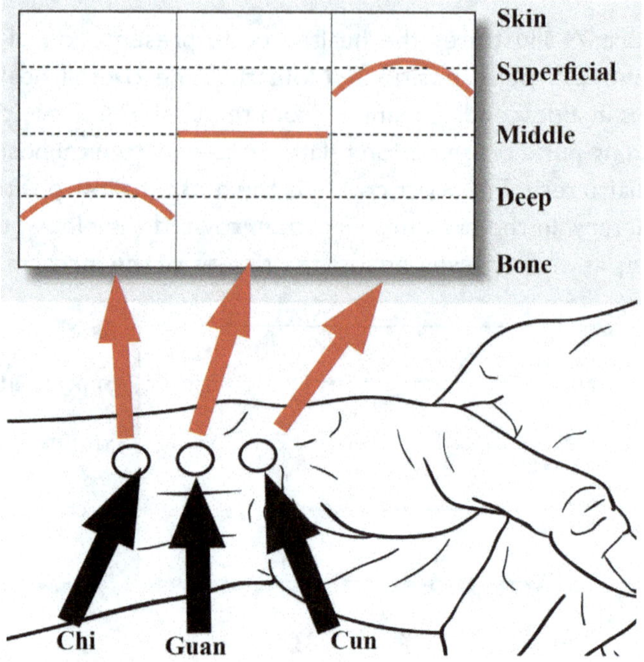

Figure 75: Proper physiological pulse depths (left hand)

The healthy pulse of each position is located in the "proper home" (physiological depth). All of the pulse positions, except the left Guan, maintain a healthy convex shape. The left Guan maintains a healthy wiry shape in the middle depth. The optimal convex pulses have a stable amplitude (neither too high or too low) and keep adequate resistance to the pressure of palpation. The healthy left Guan also maintains adequate resistance to the pressure of palpation.

The width (thick or thin) quality of the pulse is relative to the physical size and constitution of each patient. Patients with leaner body types will tend to have thinner pulses. Versus patients who have larger and more robust body types, who will tend instead to have thicker pulses. Pulse widths that are dissimilar to the patient's size and constitution exemplify a pathological condition.

The overall healthy pulse represents the optimal function of the body systems. This pulse presentation is the treatment goal for every patient.

6

Pathological (Unhealthy) Pulses - Depth, Force, and Width

Traditional pulse methods provide a general diagnosis based on the impression of the overall pulse qualities. In comparison, MPD analyzes each pulse position in impressive detail for the accurate diagnosis of multiple organ systems and anatomical regions.

In MPD, it is the combination of the pulse shape, depth, force and width that determine the specific Chinese medical and related western medical conditions. This chapter subdivides into sections that delineate the pulses and conditions based on the pulse depth, force, and width. This organization helps to discern the specific pulses more efficiently. The ensuing comparative analysis facilitates a deeper understanding of specific pathomechanisms for the guidance of effective treatment strategies. The subsequent chapter combines the pulse depth, force, and width with the distinct pulse shapes. This systematic structure directly correlates the pulse with the Chinese medical diagnosis, related western medical conditions and correct treatment strategies.

Pathological Pulse Depths

The palpation of a pulse deviated from the "proper home" represents a dysfunction of the corresponding organ systems or anatomical regions. The pathological pulses are categorized based on the palpable level of depth; either too high or too low from the "proper home." Each depth deviation represents a pathological process of the body.

Pathological High Pulses

The elevation of a pulse above the "proper home" signifies a pathological heat or dryness condition. These pathological conditions are of either excess or deficient nature. The excess conditions subdivide into Excess Heat (inflammation) and Excess Fire (severe inflammation). The deficient conditions subdivide into Deficient Heat (functional deficiency with inflammation) and Blood & Yin deficiency (anemia and fluid deficiency - associated with dryness).

The differentiation of the pathological high pulses is dependent on the specific pulse shape, force, and width. The ensuing section describes and illustrates each of the high pulses, based on the excess or deficient condition.

Excess Pathological High Pulses

1. Excess Heat (Inflammation)

Figure 76 illustrates the standard pulse representing Excess Heat. This pulse is a high, forceful, slightly thick convex pulse. In the Cun positions, the Excess Heat pulse is palpable at the skin level or superficial level. In the Guan positions, it is palpable at the superficial level. In the Chi positions, it is palpable at the middle or superficial levels.

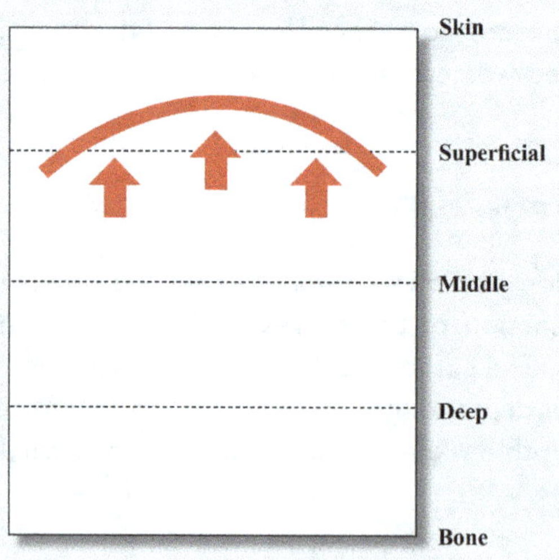

Figure 76: Excess Heat pulse (arrows denote a strong pulse force)

2. Excess Fire (Increased Inflammation)

Figure 77 illustrates the standard pulse representing Excess Fire. This pulse is a high, very forceful, thick, convex pulse with a strong/pounding quality at the skin, superficial, middle and very often the deep levels. Compared to Excess Heat, Excess Fire is a more severe pathological process and requires a stronger treatment strategy.

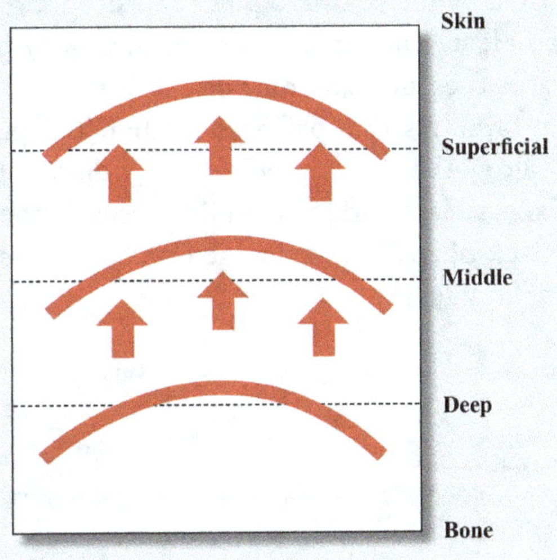

Figure 77: Excess Fire pulse (arrows denote a strong pulse force)

Deficient Pathological High Pulses

1. Yin Deficiency with Increased Heat

(Functional Deficiency - Low-Level Inflammation, Dryness)

Figure 78 illustrates the standard pulse representing Yin Deficiency with Increased Heat. This pulse is a high, thin, wiry pulse. The inflammation elevates the pulse and may display a forceful pulse quality at the superficial level. As one palpates further, the pulse force diminishes or may altogether "give way." The key differentiating factor, relative to the Excess Heat and Excess Fire pulses, is the slightly thin, wiry nature and lack of resistance. In each position, this pulse is palpable at the superficial level.

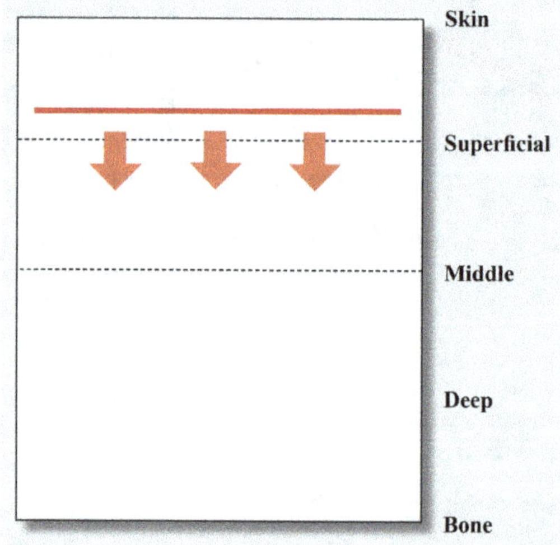

Figure 78: Yin Deficiency with Increased Heat

2. Blood & Yin Deficiency (Anemia and Fluid Deficiency/Nutrient Deficiency - Dryness, Low-Level Inflammation)

Figure **79** illustrates the standard pulse representing Blood & Yin Deficiency. This pulse is a high, forceless (weak), thin, wiry pulse. A lack of adequate resistance exemplifies the weak pulse quality. With even slight pressure, this pulse "gives way" with no perceivable pulse underneath. The overall high, thin and forceless pulse qualities relate to the severity of blood and fluid consumption by pathological dryness. Also, the dry (fluid deficient) condition, may result from acute or chronic bleeding issues that deplete fluid volume.

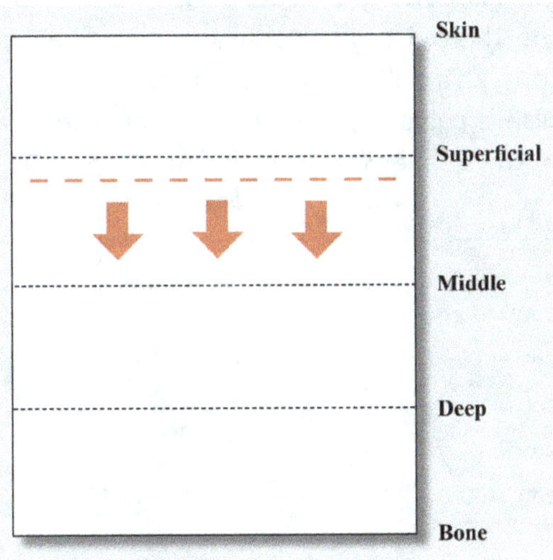

Figure 79: Blood & Yin Deficiency pulse (arrows denote a weak pulse force)

Pathological Low Pulses

The depression of a pulse below the "proper home" is due to specific excess or deficient pathological conditions. Dampness (fluid retention) and Blood Stasis (circulatory occlusion) are the excess conditions that weigh the pulses down to the deep level. The Yang

Deficiency (functional deficiency with cold) pulses also manifest below the "proper home."

The differentiation of the pathological low pulses is dependent on the specific pulse shape, force, and width. The ensuing section describes and illustrates each of the low pulses, based on the excess or deficient conditions.

Excess Pathological Low Pulses

1. Dampness (Fluid Retention)

Figure 80 illustrates the standard pulse representing Dampness (fluid retention). This pulse is a deep, slightly thick, convex pulse. In the Cun positions, this pulse is palpable at the middle or deep level. In the Guan positions, this pulse is palpable at the deep level. In the Chi position, this pulse is palpable at the bone level. The more severe the Damp condition, the deeper the pulse is found.

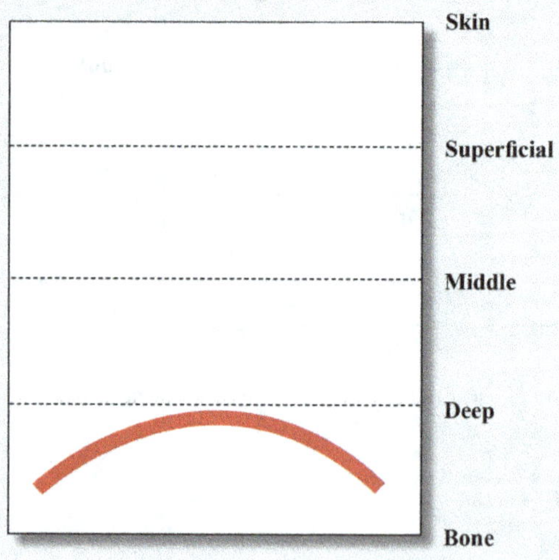

Figure 80: Dampness pulse

2. Damp-Heat (Fluid Retention and Inflammation)

Figure 81 illustrates the standard pulse representing Damp-Heat. This pulse is a deep, forceful, thick, convex or wiry pulse in the same pathological depths as the Dampness (fluid retention) pulse. Clinically, fluid retention (edema) and concurrent inflammation develop as the result of chronic circulatory obstruction.

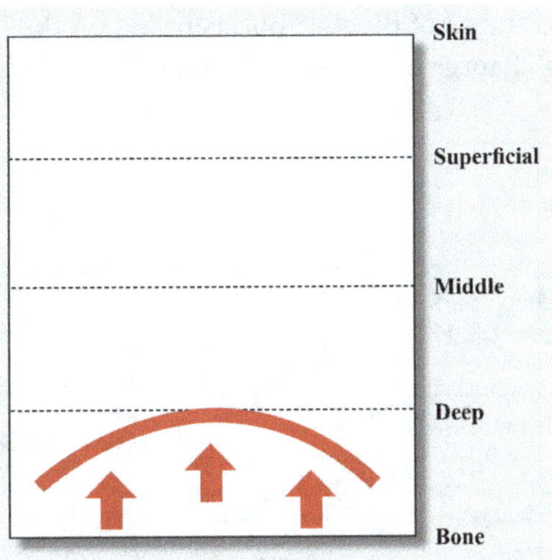

Figure 81: Damp-Heat pulse (arrows denote a strong pulse force)

3. Blood Stasis (Circulatory Obstruction)

Figure 82 illustrates the standard pulse representing Blood Stasis. Blood Stasis pulses, also termed Blocked pulses, are palpable as deep and amorphous in quality. In these cases, the radial artery lacks a defined shape and boundary. The amorphous quality compares to placing the fingers on Jello. In the Cun, Guan and Chi positions, this pulse quality is palpable at the deep level. In severe cases of Blood Stasis, the amorphous quality is perceived only at the bone level. MPD outlines three stages of Blocked pulses based on the level of severity. The following chapter details each level of Blocked pulses.

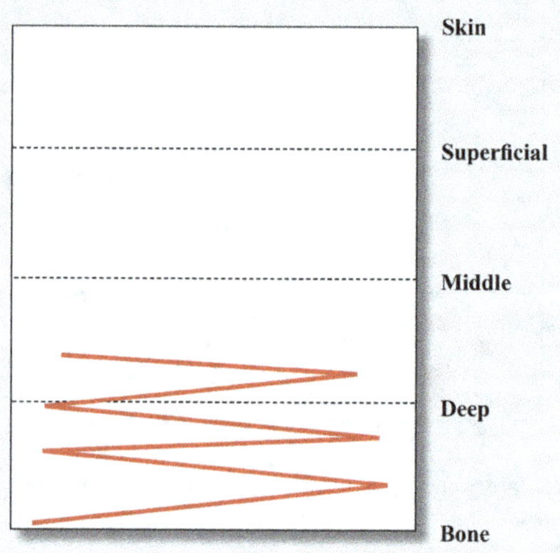

Figure 82: Blood Stasis pulse

Deficient Pathological Low Pulses

Yang Deficiency (Functional Deficiency with Cold)

Figure 83 illustrates the standard pulse representing Yang Deficiency. This pulse is a forceless (weak), thin, wiry pulse. A lack of adequate resistance exemplifies the weak pulse quality. With the application of even slight pressure, the distinct thin pulse "gives way" with no perceivable pulse underneath. In the Cun, Guan and Chi positions, this pulse is palpable at either the "proper home" or deeper levels concurrent with patient signs of fatigue, cold extremities, and pale complexion.

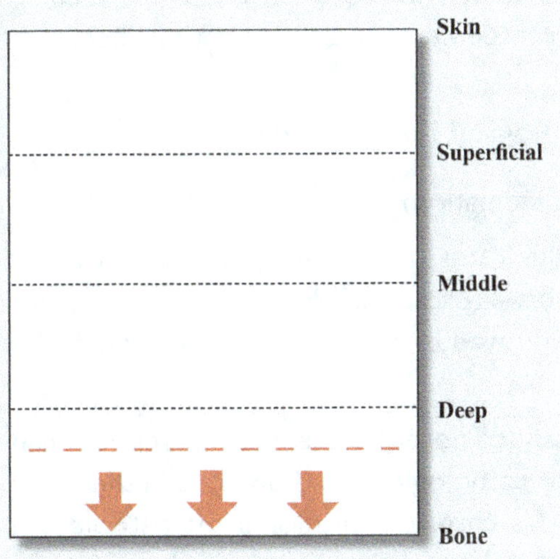

Figure 83: Yang Deficiency pulse (arrows denote a weak pulse force)

Pathological Pulse Force

The resistance level of the pulse to pressure determines the pulse force. The healthy pulses, in the "proper home," preserve a balanced level of resistance to palpation, neither too much or too little. The pulses that maintain strong resistance to pressure are pathological forceful pulses. The forceful nature reflects a pathological excess condition of either Excess Heat or Excess Cold.

In contrast, pathological forceless pulses fail to resist pressure and "give way" with no perceivable pulse underneath. The forceless nature reflects a pathological deficient condition of either Qi Deficiency, Yang deficiency, Blood Deficiency, Yin Deficiency, Yin Deficiency with Increased Heat or a combination thereof.

Excess Pathological Forceful Pulses

1. Heat (Inflammation)

Figure 84 illustrates the forceful pulse quality associated with Excess Heat. In this illustration Excess Heat is the primary pathological condition indicated by the high, slightly thick convex and forceful pulse.

It is important to note that Heat (inflammation) can manifest concurrent to other pathological conditions, as in the case of Damp-Heat (figure 85). In this case, the predominant pathology is Blood Stasis (circulatory occlusion) and Dampness (fluid retention). The Heat (inflammation) gives the pulse a forceful quality, but the pulse remains in the deep level due to the dominant Blood Stasis and Dampness conditions.

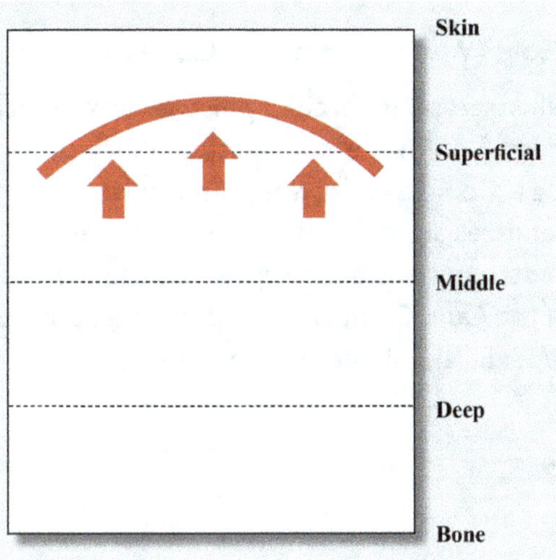

Figure 84: Excess Heat pulse (arrows denote a strong pulse force)

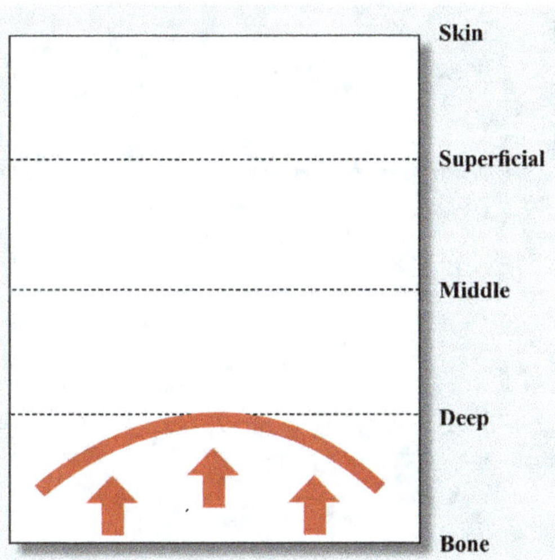

Figure 85: Damp-Heat pulse (arrows denote a strong pulse force)

2. Excess Cold (Vasoconstriction - Cold)

Figure 86 illustrates the forceful pulse quality associated with Excess Cold. Excess Cold has a contracting effect on the vasculature, which reflects as a constricted, very thin pulse of hard quality that maintains forceful resistance to pressure. Harder and thinner pulse qualities with a strong resistance represent the increased severity of Excess Cold. In the Cun, Guan and Chi positions, this pulse is palpable at either the superficial, middle or deep levels.

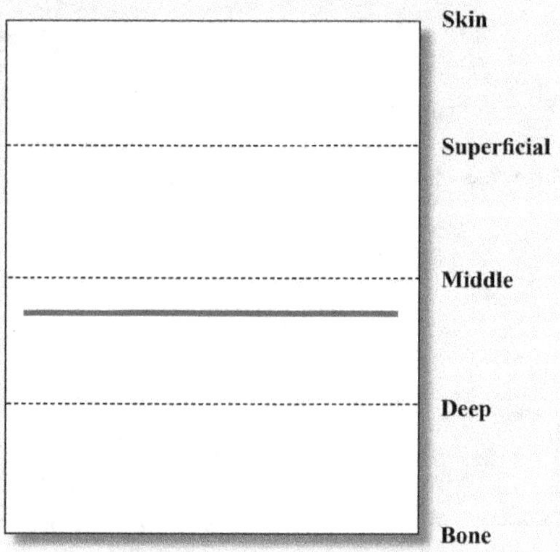

Figure 86: Excess Cold pulse

Deficient Pathological Forceless Pulses

1. Qi Deficiency (Functional Deficiency)

Figure 87 illustrates the forceless quality associated with Qi Deficiency. This pulse is a slightly thick, convex or wiry pulse lacking sufficient durability to pressure. With the application of slight pressure, the thick outer-barrier compresses, giving the perception of a hollow interior vessel space. Palpating this pulse is similar to pressing on the outer barrier of a scallion stalk. This pulse is uncommon considering Qi deficiency often occurs in combination with other deficiency patterns. In the Cun, Guan and Chi positions, this pulse is palpable at either the superficial, middle or deep levels.

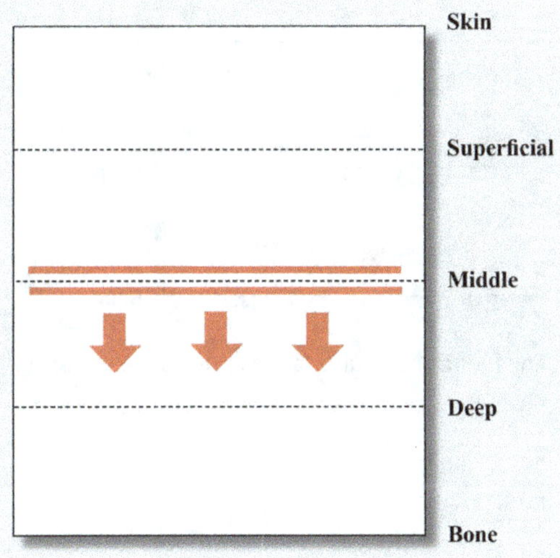

Figure 87: Qi Deficiency pulse

2. Yang deficiency (Functional Deficiency with Cold)

Figure 88 illustrates the forceless quality associated with Yang Deficiency. This pulse is a forceless, thin, wiry pulse. With the application of even slight pressure, the distinct thin pulse "gives way" with no perceivable pulse underneath. In the Cun, Guan and Chi positions, this pulse is palpable at the "proper home" or deeper levels concurrent with patient signs of fatigue, cold extremities, and pale complexion.

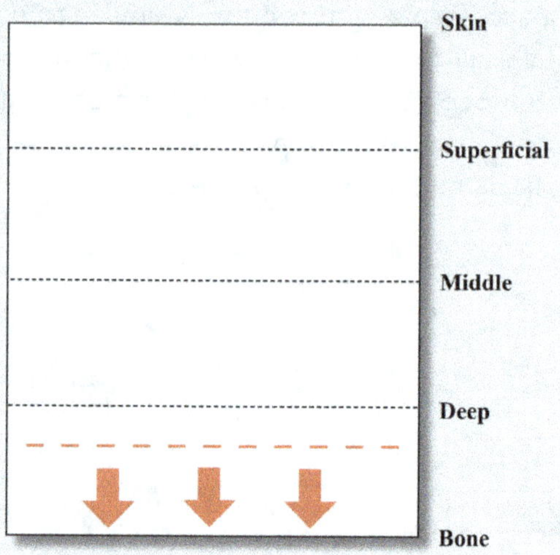

Figure 88: Yang Deficiency pulse (arrows denote a weak pulse force)

3. Blood Deficiency

(Anemia, Fluid Deficiency/Nutrient Deficiency & Blood Loss)

Figure **89** illustrates the forceless quality associated with Blood Deficiency. This pulse is a forceless, thin, wiry pulse. With even slight pressure, the pulse "gives way" with no perceivable pulse underneath. The thin and weak qualities relate to the severity of decreased blood volume. In the Cun, Guan and Chi positions, the Blood Deficiency pulse usually appears above the designated "proper home." Blood Deficiency (anemia) often occurs in combination with Yin Deficiency (fluid deficiency) and combine for a forceless, thin, wiry pulse at the superficial level.

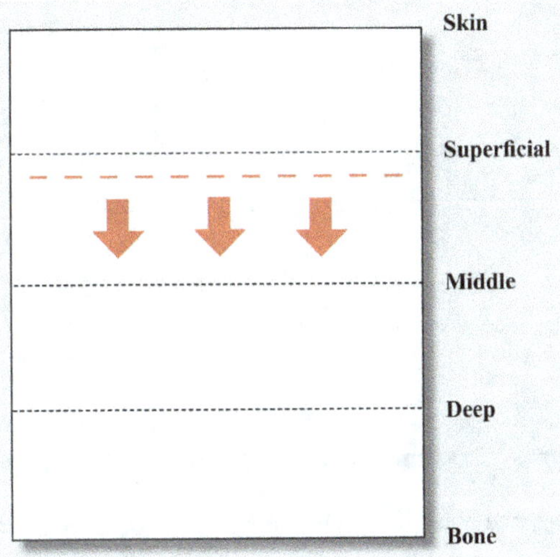

Figure 89: Blood Deficiency pulse (arrows denote a weak pulse force)

4. Yin Deficiency

(Fluid Deficiency - Dryness, Low-level Inflammation)

Figure 90 illustrates the forceless quality associated with Yin Deficiency. This pulse is a high, forceless, thin, wiry pulse. With even slight pressure, this pulse also "gives way" with no perceivable pulse underneath. The overall high, thin, and weak pulse qualities relate to the severity of fluid consumption by pathological dryness. In each pulse position, the Yin Deficiency pulse appears most often at the superficial level, though in the Chi position it can present at the middle level.

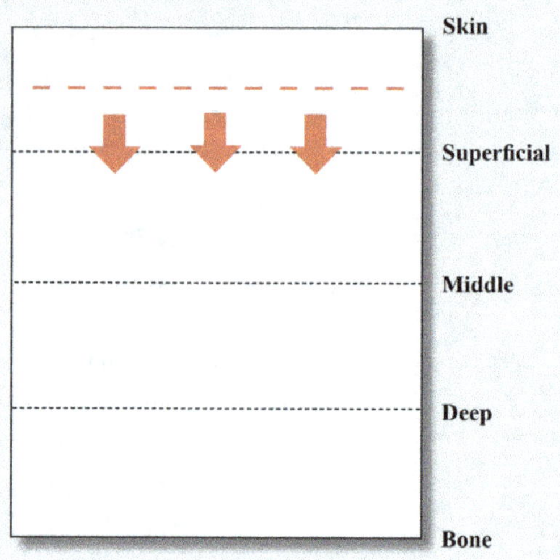

Figure 90: Yin Deficiency pulse (Fluid Deficiency - Dryness, Low-level inflammation)

5. Yin Deficiency with Increased Heat

(Functional Deficiency - Low-Level Inflammation, Dryness)

Figure 91 illustrates the unique forceless quality associated with Yin Deficiency with Increased Heat. This pulse is a high, thin, wiry pulse. The inflammation elevates the pulse and may initially display a forceful pulse quality at the superficial level. As one palpates further, the pulse force diminishes or may altogether "give way." Due to the increased inflammation, this pulse is slightly more forceful and wider than the previous Yin Deficiency pulse. In each pulse position, Yin deficiency with increased Heat is a pulse that is palpable at the superficial level.

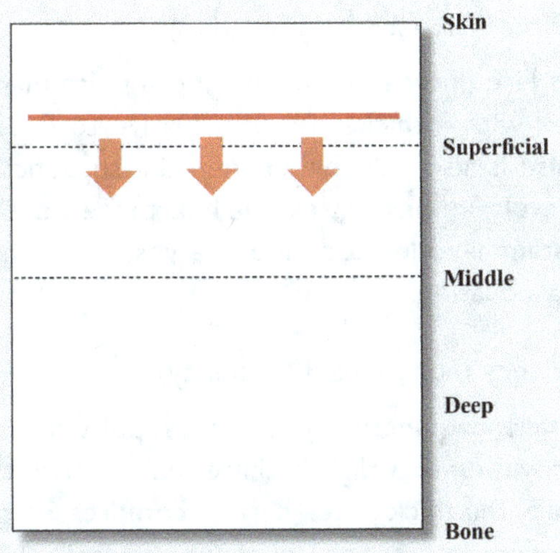

Figure 91: Yin Deficiency with Increased Heat pulse

Assessment of the Two Widths

As mentioned earlier the healthy width (thick or thin) quality of the pulse is relative to the physical size and constitution of each patient. Pulses that are too thick, relative to the patient's size, are the result of either Excess Heat, Excess Fire or Qi Deficiency. Thin pulses, relative to the patient size, that maintain resistance to pressure are due to Excess Cold or Severe Blood Stasis with Excess Cold. Thin pulses that "give way" with pressure are due to Yang Deficiency, Blood Deficiency, Yin Deficiency, or Deficient Heat.

Pathological Thick Pulses

1. Excess Heat (Inflammation)

The Excess Heat (inflammation) pulse manifests as high, forceful and convex with a slightly thick quality. In general, inflammation causes increased blood circulation and blood volume production, as well as adaptations to the pumping mechanism of the heart. The heart rate and systemic blood pressure become slightly elevated, which lead to inevitable compensation of the vessel wall.

2. Excess Fire (Increased Inflammation)

The Excess Fire (increased inflammation) pulse manifests as high, forceful, convex with a thicker quality relative to Excess Heat. The Excess Fire pulse is also palpable in the skin, superficial, middle and possibly deep levels. In these cases, the heart rate and blood pressure are more substantially elevated, and the vessel wall has undergone more severe vasodilation.

3. Qi Deficiency (Functional Deficiency)

The Qi Deficiency (functional deficiency) pulse manifests as forceless, convex or wiry with a slightly thick quality. With the application of slight pressure, the thick outer-barrier compresses, giving the perception of a hollow interior vessel space. Overall, this pulse is uncommon considering Qi deficiency often occurs in combination with other deficiency patterns. This same pulse quality manifests in cases of severe acute blood loss. In these cases, the blood volume drastically decreases, yet the blood vessel maintains the normal structure. The slightly thick vessel wall easily collapses due to the diminished blood supply.

Pathological Thin Pulses

1. Excess Cold (Vasoconstriction - Cold)

The Excess Cold pulse manifests as a very thin pulse that maintains resistance to pressure. Excess Cold has a contracting effect on the vasculature leading to the hard and thin pulse quality. The thin Excess Cold pulse keeps resistance to pressure, while the thin deficient pulses do not.

2. Blood Stasis with Excess Cold

(Vasoconstriction - Tension and Cold)

The Blood Stasis with Excess Cold pulse manifests as a hard, thin pulse at depth. In each position, this pulse presents deeper than the "proper home". In these cases, the vasculature is constricted due to excessive sympathetic nervous system activity. The increased tension of the vessels impedes efficient blood circulation to the corresponding organs/anatomical regions. The restricted circulation is associated with decreased nourishment and warmth to the area, increasing the susceptibility to Excess Cold conditions. The established Excess Cold further constricts the vasculature.

3. Yang Deficiency (Functional Deficiency with Cold)

The Yang Deficiency pulse manifests as a very thin pulse that "gives way" to pressure with no perceivable pulse underneath. These pulses represent a degree of organ deterioration and loss of function over a prolonged period. Chronic vasoconstriction due to Excess Cold and/ or Blood Stasis reduces optimal blood circulation, which eventually leads to the weakened organ function.

4. Blood Deficiency

(Anemia, Fluid Deficiency/Nutrient Deficiency & Blood Loss)

The Blood Deficiency pulse is also a thin pulse that "gives way" to pressure with no perceivable pulse underneath. In the Cun, Guan and Chi positions, the Blood Deficiency pulse usually appears above the designated proper "home." These pulses represent the diminished circulation of blood and nutrient factors due to either genetic predisposition, poor dietary nutrient absorption or bleeding issues.

5. Yin Deficiency

(Fluid Deficiency - Dryness, Low-level Inflammation)

The Yin Deficiency pulse manifests as an elevated thin pulse that "gives way" to pressure with no perceivable pulse underneath. In each pulse position, the Yin Deficiency pulse appears most often at the superficial level, though in the Chi position it can present at the middle level. The overall high, thin, and forceless pulse qualities relate to the severity of fluid consumption by pathological dryness.

6. Yin Deficiency with Increased Heat

(Functional Deficiency - Low-Level Inflammation, Dryness)

The Yin Deficiency with Increased Heat pulse is an elevated thin pulse that displays initial resistance at the superficial level. With deeper palpation, the pulse force diminishes or may altogether "give way." The increased inflammation makes this pulse slightly more forceful and wider than the previous Yin Deficiency pulse and requires a distinct treatment approach.

7

Pathological (Unhealthy) Pulses - Combination of Shape, Depth, Force, Width & Systemic Pulses

There are five basic pulse shapes which provide critical diagnostic information in combination with the pulse depth, force, and width.

The five pulse shapes:

1. Convex Pulses

2. Wiry Pulses

3. Blocked Pulses

4. Compressed Pulses

5. Systemic Pulses

The convex, wiry and blocked pulse shapes are a significant component in determining the correct MPD diagnosis. The combination of these pulse shapes with specific pathological pulse depths, levels of resistance (force) and pathological pulse widths accurately establishes the diagnosis and relevant treatment strategy. The following sections categorize each of the potential pulse quality combinations associated with the convex, wiry and blocked pulses. The understanding of these pulse qualities and specific conditions is then efficiently adapted to the corresponding organ systems and anatomical regions of the particular Cun, Guan, Chi, Proximal and additional Cun "valley" pulses. For example, the Deep - Forceful - Thin - Wiry pulse represents Blood Stasis with Excess Cold. When located in the left Chi and Proximal position on a female patient, this pulse quality represents Blood Stasis with Excess Cold affecting the reproductive system. These patients manifest with the pain and menstrual symptoms associated with endometriosis.

In the following descriptions, the depth (high or low) denotes the pulse location relative to the proper "home" level. For example, the proper "home" of the Guan positions is the middle level. In respect to the Guan positions, the High - Forceful - Slightly Thick - Convex pulse is palpable in the superficial level or potentially the skin level. The Low - Forceful - Slightly Thick - Convex Pulse is palpable at the deep level or between the deep and bone levels.

Convex Pulses

The healthy convex pulse is the physiological shape of all the pulse positions, except the left Guan (figures 92 & 93).

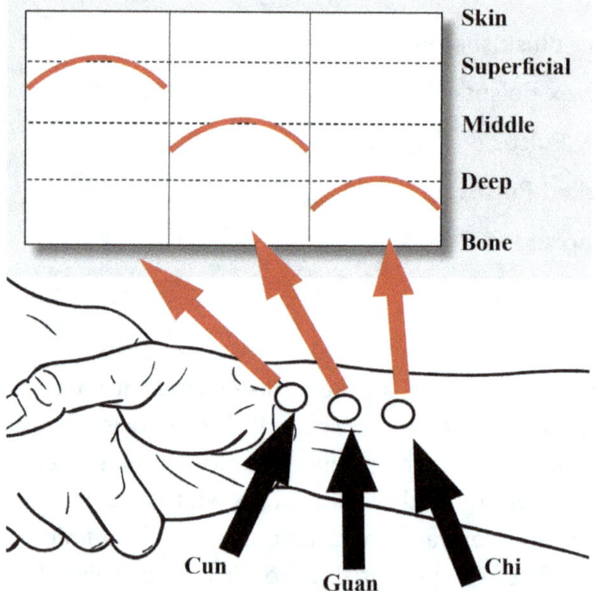

Figure 92: Proper physiological convex pulses (right hand)

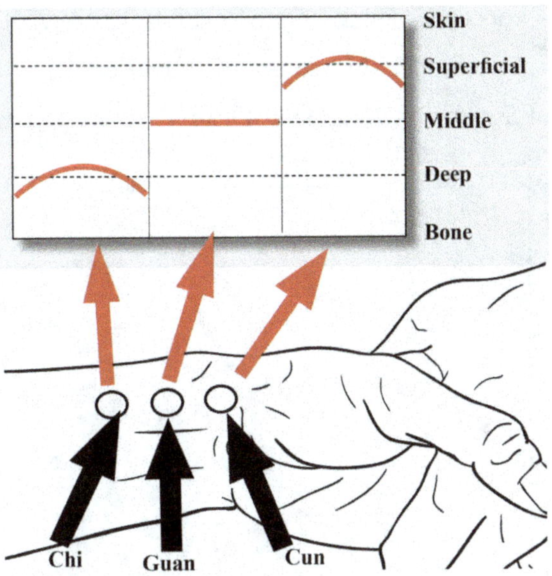

Figure 93: Proper physiological pulse shapes (left hand)

Pathological High - Convex Pulses

Ia . High - Forceful - Slightly Thick - Convex pulse (figure 94):

Diagnosis: Excess Heat (Inflammation)

Treatment Strategy: Clear Heat - 100%

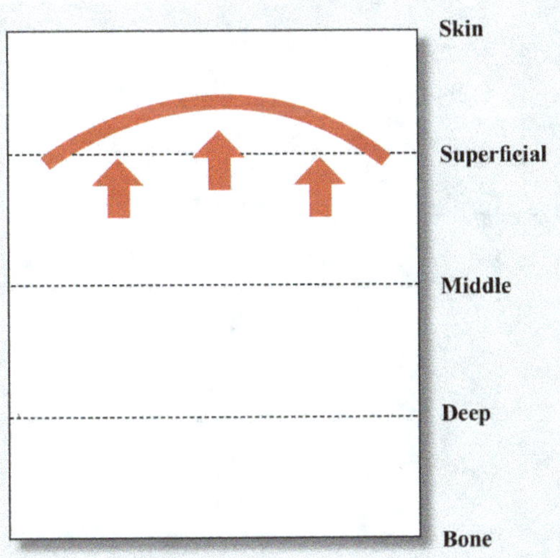

Figure 94: Excess Heat pulse (arrows denote a strong pulse force)

Ib. High - Forceful - Thick - Convex pulse (figure 95):

Diagnosis: Excess Fire (Increased Inflammation)

Treatment Strategy: Clear Heat, Drain Fire - 100%

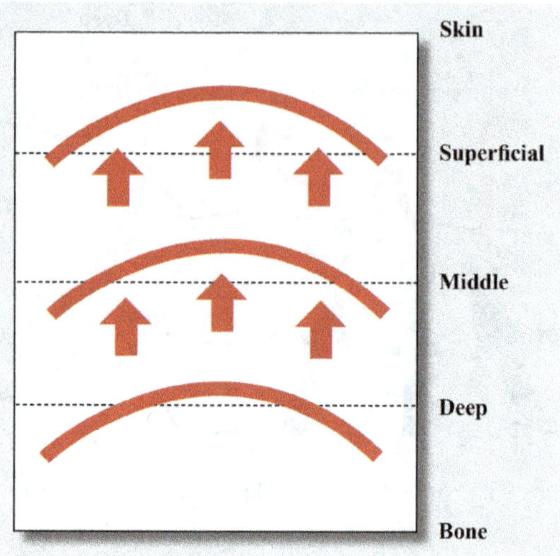

Figure 95: Excess Fire pulse (arrows denote a strong pulse force)

2. High - Forceful - Thin - Convex pulse (figure 96):

Diagnosis: Excess Heat (Inflammation) & Secondary Stagnation (Vaso-constriction/Arteriosclerosis/Atherosclerosis)

Treatment Strategy: Clear Heat - 80% / Disperse Stagnation - 20%

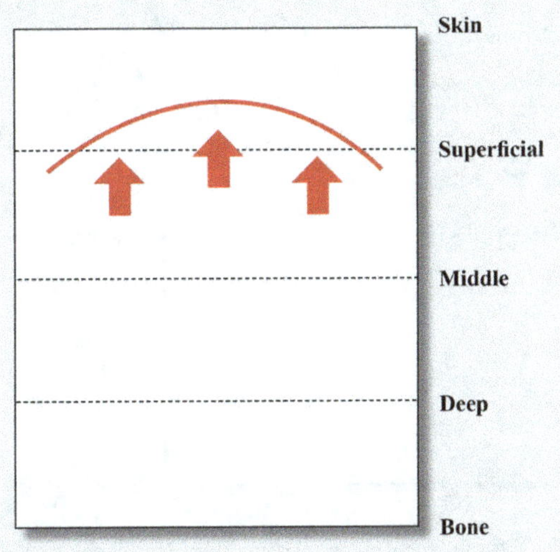

Figure 96: Excess Heat & Secondary Stagnation pulse
(arrows denote a strong pulse force)

3. High - Forceless - Slightly Thick - Convex Pulse (figure 97) :

Diagnosis: Qi Deficiency (Functional Deficiency)

Treatment Strategy: Tonify Qi - 100%

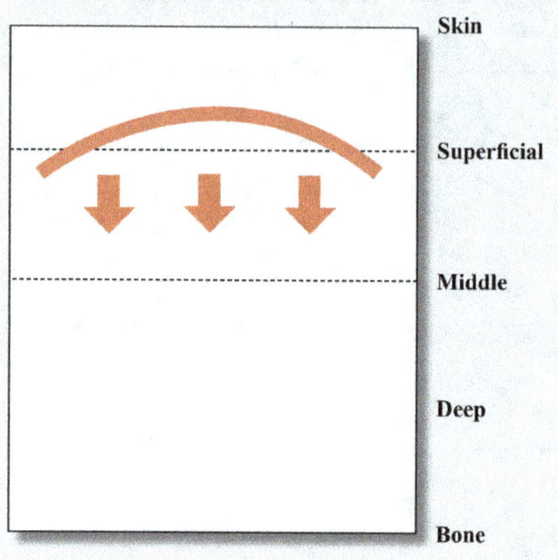

Figure 97: Qi Deficiency pulse (arrows denote a weak pulse force)

4. High - Forceless - Slightly Thin - Convex Pulse (figure 98):

Diagnosis: Blood Deficiency (Anemia, Fluid Deficiency/Nutrient Deficiency & Blood Loss) & Secondary Dryness (Fluid Deficiency) with Qi Deficiency (Functional Deficiency)

Treatment Strategy: Nourish Blood - 70% / Moisten Dryness - 20% / Tonify Qi - 10%

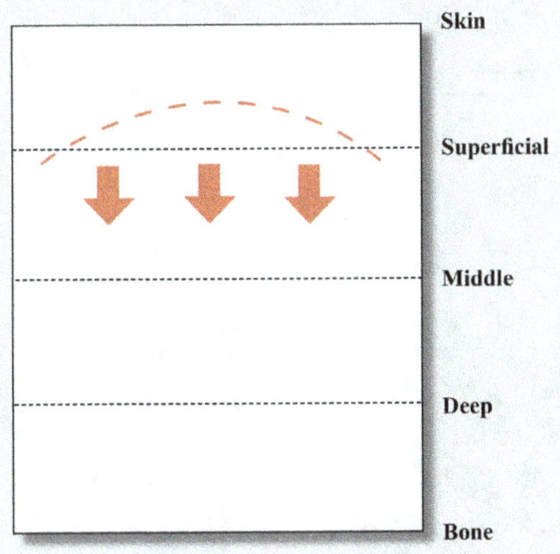

Figure 98: Blood Deficiency & Secondary Dryness pulse
(arrows denote a weak pulse force)

Pathological Low - Convex Pulses

I. Low - Forceful - Slightly Thick - Convex Pulse (figure 99):

Diagnosis: Blood Stasis (Circulatory Obstruction) & Damp-Heat (Fluid Retention and Inflammation)

Treatment Strategy: Invigorate Blood - 70-80% / Clear Heat & Eliminate Dampness - 20-30%

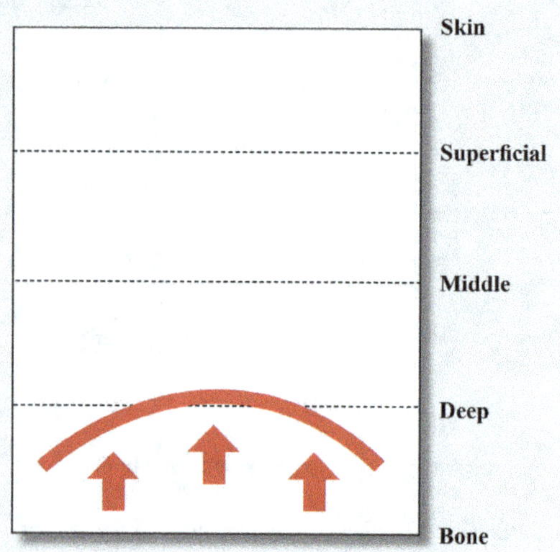

Figure 99: Blood Stasis & Damp-Heat pulse (arrows denote a strong pulse force)

2. Low - Forceful - Thin - Convex Pulse (figure 100):

Diagnosis: Blood Stasis (Circulatory Occlusion) / Dampness (Fluid Retention) & Secondary Excess Cold (Vasoconstriction)

Treatment Strategy: Invigorate Blood - 80% / Dispel Cold - 20%

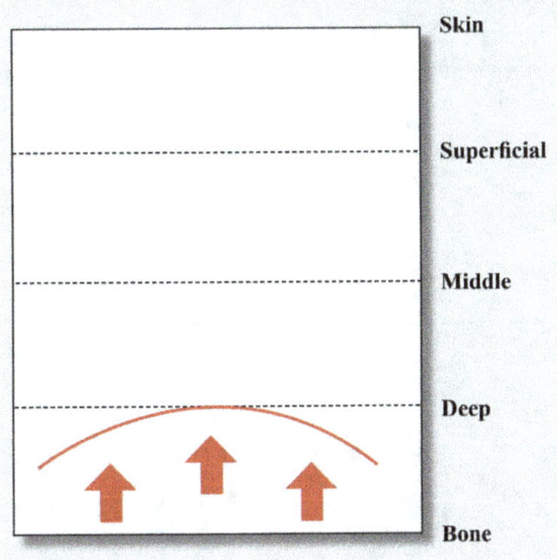

Figure 100: Blood Stasis / Dampness & Secondary Excess Cold pulse
(arrows denote a strong pulse force)

3. Low - Forceless - Slightly Thick - Convex Pulse (figure 101):

Diagnosis: Blood Stasis (Circulatory Occlusion) / Dampness (Fluid Retention) & Qi Deficiency (Functional Deficiency)

Treatment Strategy: Invigorate Blood - 70% / Tonify Qi - 20% / Resolve Dampness - 10%

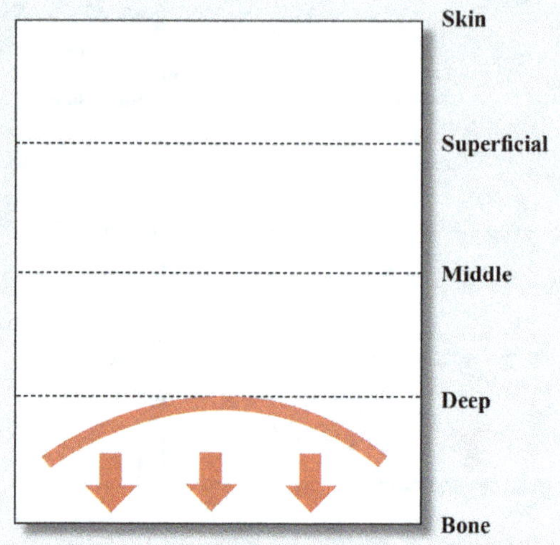

Figure 101: Blood Stasis / Dampness & Qi Deficiency pulse
(arrows denote a weak pulse force)

4. Low - Forceless - Slightly Thin - Convex Pulse (figure 102):

Diagnosis: Blood Stasis (Circulatory Occlusion) / Dampness (Fluid Retention) & Yang Deficiency (Functional Deficiency with Cold)

Treatment Strategy: Invigorate Blood - 80% / Tonify Yang - 20 %

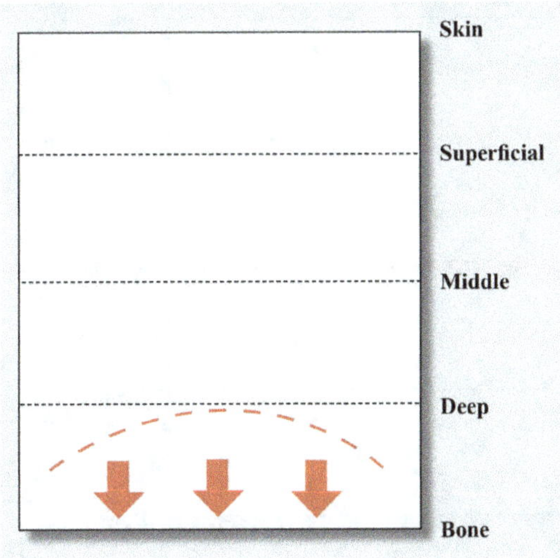

Figure 102: Blood Stasis / Dampness & Yang Deficiency pulse
(arrows denote a weak pulse force)

Wiry Pulses

The healthy wiry pulse is the physiological shape of the left Guan position (figure 103).

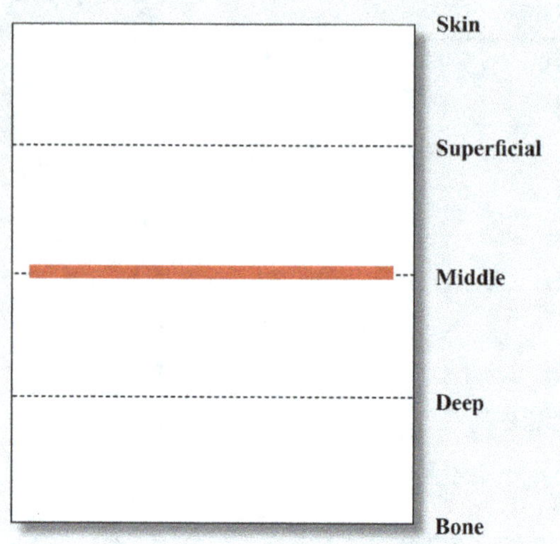

Figure 103: Healthy wiry pulse in the left Guan position

Specific to the right Cun, the High - Wiry pulse represents an active immune system engagement (Wind Invasion). In these cases, the immune system responds to specific pathogenic invasions (e.g. common cold/airborne allergens). A High - Forceful - Slightly Thick - Wiry pulse indicates an inflammatory immune response (Wind-Heat condition). A High - Forceful - Thin - Wiry pulse indicates an immune response of less severity and cold signs (Wind-Cold condition). A High - Forceless - Thin - Wiry pulse indicates a weakened immune system, susceptible to persistent sickness and allergies.

Pathological High - Wiry Pulses

1. High - Forceful - Slightly Thick - Wiry Pulse (figure 104):

Diagnosis: Excess Heat (Inflammation) & Secondary Stagnation (Vaso-constriction/Arteriosclerosis/Atherosclerosis)

Treatment Strategy: Clear Heat - 80% / Disperse Stagnation - 20%

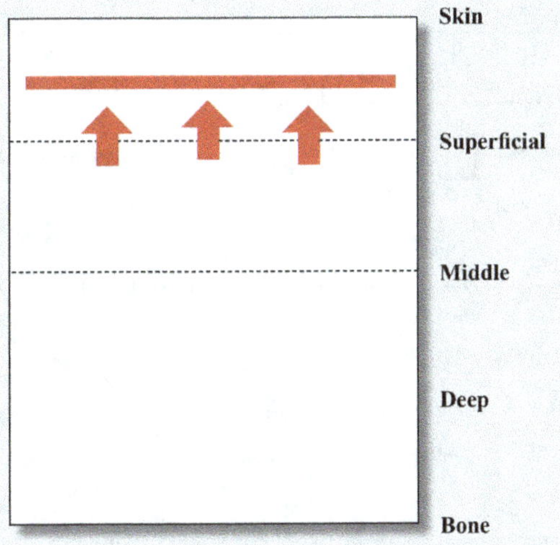

Figure 104: Excess Heat & Secondary Stagnation pulse
(arrows denote a strong pulse force)

2. High - Forceful - Thin - Wiry Pulse (figure 105):

Diagnosis: Excess Heat (Inflammation) shifting to Yin deficiency with increased Heat (Functional Deficiency - Low-Level Inflammation, Dryness) & Secondary Stagnation (Vasoconstriction/Arteriosclerosis/Atherosclerosis)

Treatment Strategy: Nourish Yin - 70% / Clear Heat - 20% / Disperse Stagnation - 10%

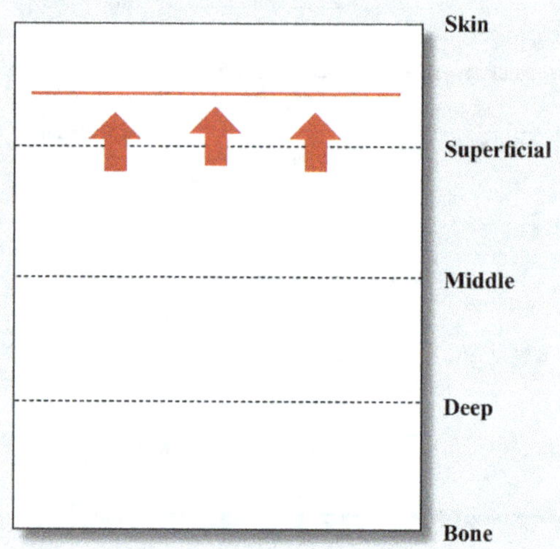

Figure 105: Excess Heat shifting to Yin Def. with Increased Heat & Secondary Stagnation pulse (arrows denote a strong pulse force)

3. High - Forceless - Slightly Thick - Wiry Pulse (figure 106):

Diagnosis: Qi deficiency (Functional Deficiency) with Heat (Inflammation) & Secondary Stagnation (Vasoconstriction/Arteriosclerosis/Atherosclerosis)

Treatment Strategy: Clear Heat - 60% / Tonify Qi - 20% / Disperse Stagnation - 20%

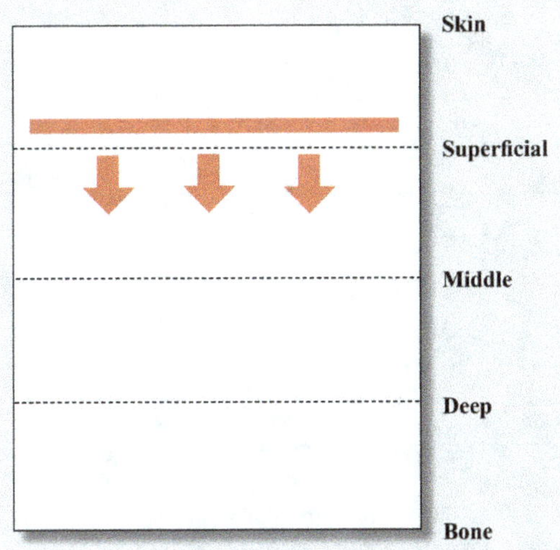

Figure 106: Qi Deficiency with Heat & Secondary Stagnation pulse (arrows denote a weak pulse force)

4. High - Forceless - Thin - Wiry Pulse (figure 107):

Diagnosis: Yin Deficiency
(Fluid Deficiency - Dryness, Low-level inflammation)

Treatment Strategy: Nourish Yin - 100%

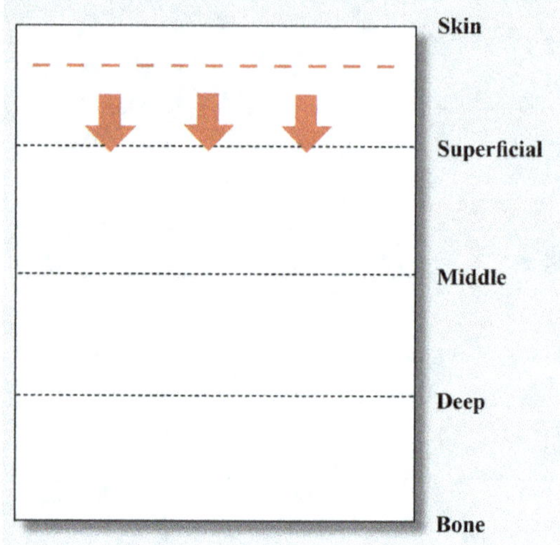

Figure 107: Yin Deficiency pulse
(arrows denote a weak pulse force)

Pathological Low - Wiry Pulses

1. Low - Forceful - Slightly Thick - Wiry Pulse (figure 108):

Diagnosis: Blood Stasis (Circulatory Occlusion) & Secondary Damp-Heat (Fluid Retention and Inflammation)

Treatment Strategy: Invigorate Blood - 70% / Clear Heat & Eliminate Dampness - 30%

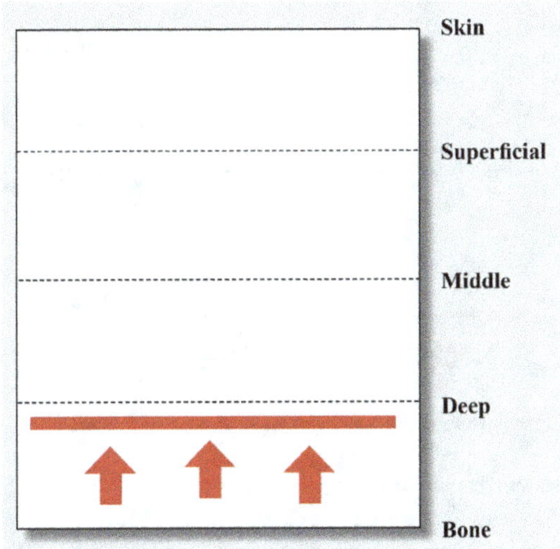

Figure 108: Blood Stasis & Secondary Damp-Heat pulse
(arrows denote a strong pulse force)

2. Low - Forceful - Thin - Wiry Pulse (figure 109):

Diagnosis: Blood Stasis (Circulatory Occlusion) & Secondary Excess Cold (Vasoconstriction) with Dampness (Fluid Retention)

Treatment Strategy: Invigorate Blood - 70% /
Dispel Cold and Damp - 30%

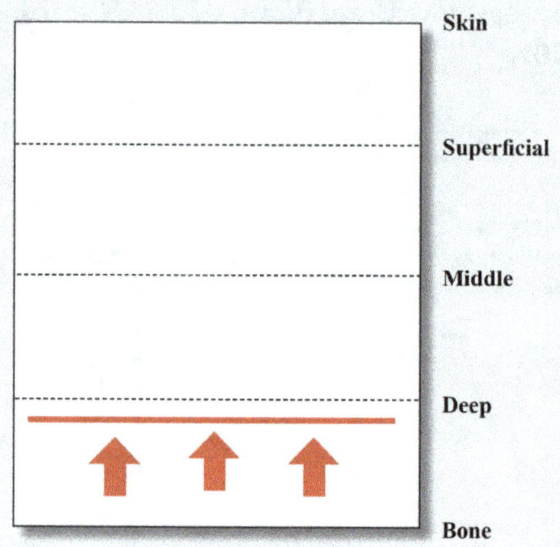

Figure 109: Blood Stasis & Secondary Excess Cold with Dampness pulse
(arrows denote a strong pulse force)

3. Low - Forceless - Slightly Thick - Wiry Pulse (figure 110):

Diagnosis: Blood Stasis (Circulatory Occlusion) / Qi deficiency (Functional Deficiency) & Secondary Dampness (Fluid Retention)

Treatment Strategy: Invigorate Blood - 80% / Tonify Qi and Eliminate Dampness - 20%

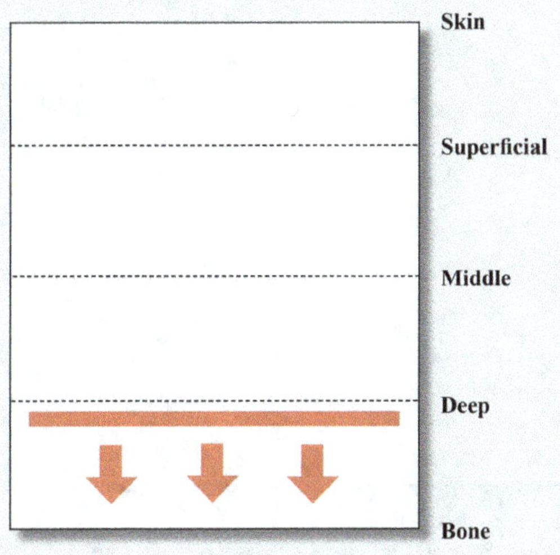

Figure 110: Blood Stasis / Qi deficiency & Secondary Dampness pulse
(arrows denote a weak pulse force)

4. Low - Forceless - Thin - Wiry Pulse (figure 111):

Diagnosis: Blood Stasis (Circulatory Occlusion) /
Yang Deficiency (Functional Deficiency with Cold)

Treatment Strategy: Invigorate Blood - 70% / Tonify Yang - 30%

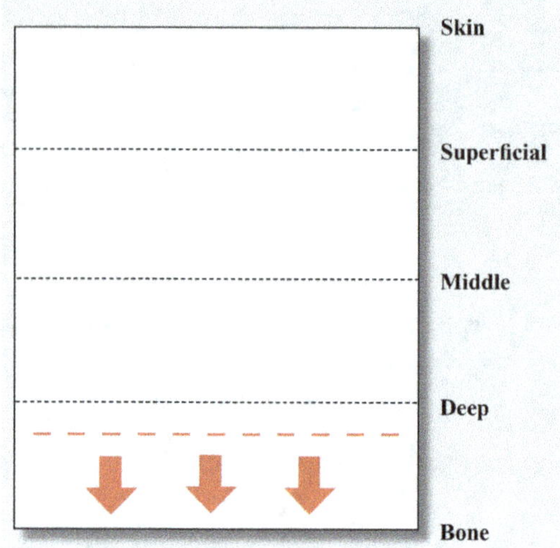

Figure 111: Blood Stasis & Yang Deficiency pulse (arrows denote a weak pulse force)

Blocked Pulses - Blood Stasis (Circulatory Occlusion)

Definitive Blood Stasis pulses are palpable as deep and amorphous in quality. In these cases, the radial artery lacks definite shape and boundaries. The amorphous quality compares to placing the fingers on Jello.

The Blocked pulses represent varying levels of Blood Stasis (Circulatory Occlusion) and Dampness (Fluid Retention). Blood stasis translates as macro- and micro-circulation obstruction. Commonly, fluid retention is a result of circulatory occlusion, though much depends on the context of the patient's condition. For each patient, the overall pulse presentation and concurrent signs/symptoms determine the proportions of Blood Stasis and Dampness.

The Blocked pulses are categorized on a scale of 1 to 3, relative to the palpable quality of blockage. Each stage represents a certain level of circulatory occlusion, and treating Blocked pulses stages 2-3 requires stronger blood invigorating herbal strategies.

1a. Stage 1 Blocked Pulse (figure 112):

The Stage 1 Blocked pulse represents **20-30** percent circulatory occlusion. In all pulse positions, the pulse is located at the deep level, and the pulse form and boundaries are only **50-70** percent palpable.

Treatment Strategy: Invigorate Blood - 100%

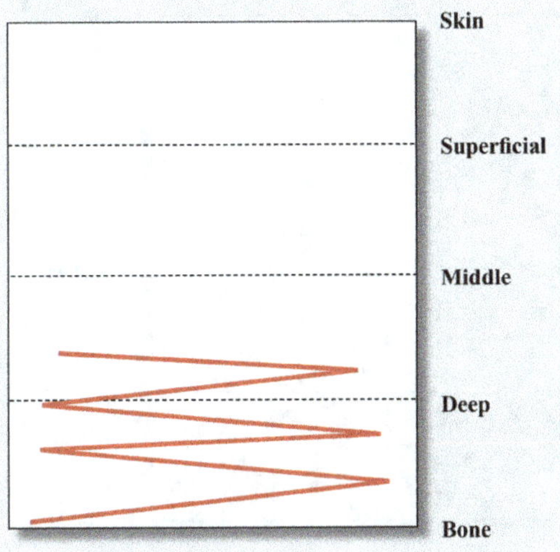

Figure 112: Stage 1 Blocked pulse

1b. Stage 2 Blocked Pulse (figure 113):

The Stage 2 Blocked pulse represents 30-50 percent circulatory occlusion. In all pulse positions, the pulse is located at the deep level, and the pulse boundaries are only 30-50 percent palpable.

Treatment Strategy: Invigorate Blood - 100%

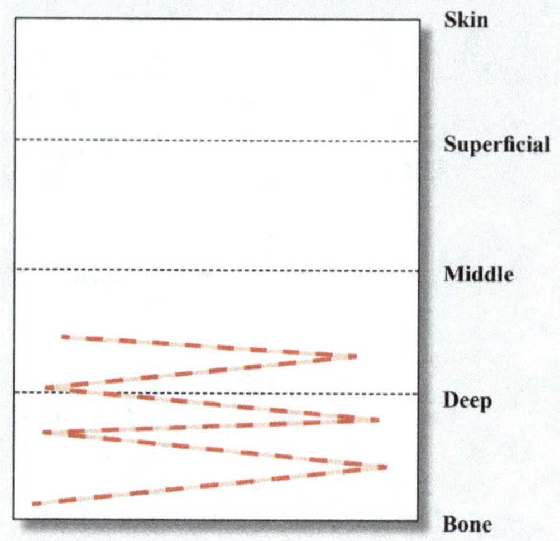

Figure 113: Stage 2 Blocked pulse

1c. Stage 3 Blocked Pulse (figure 114):

The Stage 3 Blocked pulse represents 50-plus percent circulatory occlusion. In all pulse positions, this pulse is located at the deep level, and the pulse boundaries are less than 20 percent palpable.

Treatmeunt Strategy: Invigorate Blood - 100%

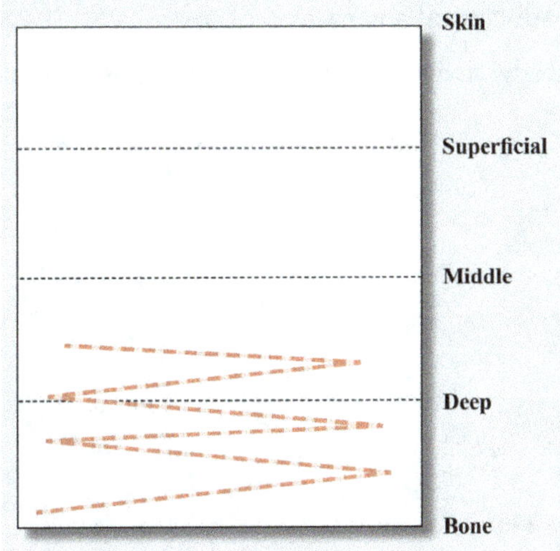

Figure 114: Stage 3 Blocked pulse

2. Blood Stasis with Excess Cold Pulse (figure 115):

The Blood Stasis (Circulatory Occlusion) with Excess Cold (Vaso-constriction) pulse manifests as a very thin, slightly hard pulse that is located within the deep Blocked pulse. In all pulse positions, this pulse is located at the deep level and may occur with any stage of Blocked pulses. This pulse is often found in the left Cun position in patients with clinical or subclinical angina pectoris.

Treatment Strategy: Invigorate Blood - 80% / Dispel Cold - 20%

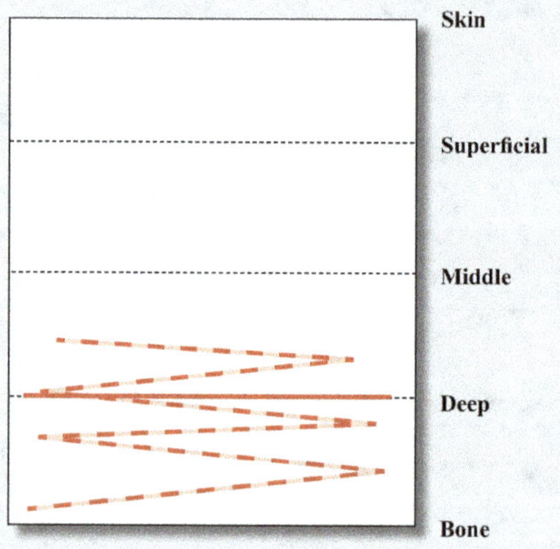

Figure 115: Blood Stasis with Excess Cold pulse

3. Blood Stasis with Yang Deficiency Pulse (figure 116):

The Blood Stasis (Circulatory Occlusion) with Yang Deficiency (Functional Deficiency with Cold) pulse manifests as a very thin pulse that "gives way" to pressure and is located within the deep Blocked pulse. In all pulse positions, this pulse is located at the deep level and may occur with any stage of Blocked pulses. These pulses represent a degree of organ deterioration and loss of function over a prolonged period. Chronic vasoconstriction due to Blood Stasis reduces optimal blood circulation, which eventually leads to the weakened organ function manifesting with signs of fatigue, cold extremities, and pale complexion.

Treatment Strategy: Invigorate Blood - 70% / Tonify Yang - 30 %

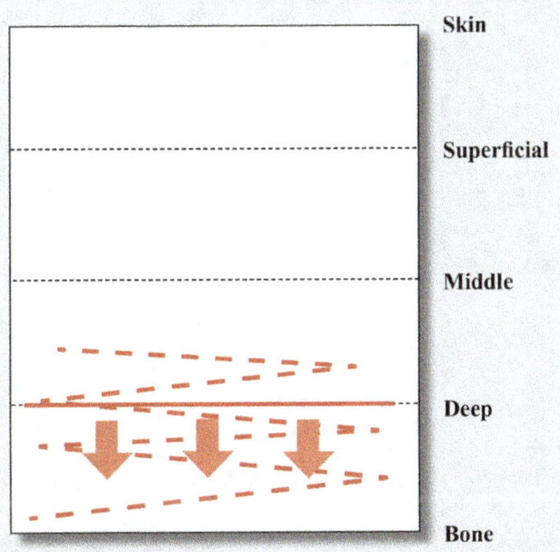

Figure 116: Blood Stasis with Yang Deficiency pulse
(arrows denote a weak pulse force)

4. Blood Stasis with Qi & Blood Deficiency Pulse (figure 117):

The Blood Stasis (Circulatory Occlusion) with Qi Deficiency (Functional Deficiency) and Blood Deficiency (Anemia, Fluid Deficiency, Nutrient Deficiency) pulse represents circulatory occlusion concurrent with deficient organ function. This pulse is often palpable in the left Cun position corresponding to the heart. Over time, the restricted circulation decreases nutritive factors to the heart and eventually leads to deficient cardiac function. This pulse is distinctly palpable as an amorphous, Jello-like quality that completely "gives way" with light pressure. The position then feels like a hollow space, empty of any other perceivable pulse qualities.

Treatment Strategy: Invigorate Blood - 70-80% /

Tonify Qi and Nourish Blood - 20-30%

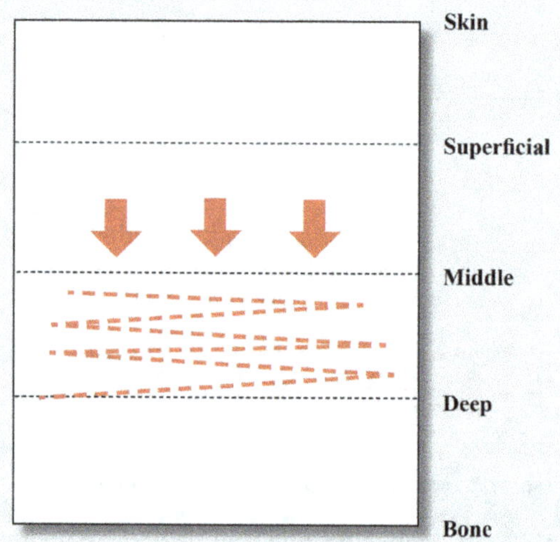

Figure 117: Blood Stasis with Qi and Blood Deficiency pulse
(arrows denote a weak pulse force)

Compressed Pulses

The Compressed pulses represent tissue aggregations that obstruct optimal blood circulation to specific organ systems and anatomical regions. These pulses maintain a markedly convex presentation and are classified based on relative size and degree of firmness. The location of the Compressed pulses is within the various fascial tissue layers intimately connected with the radial artery. These findings do not maintain a pulse wave pattern but rather integrate with the specific wave pattern of the radial pulse. In each pulse position, it is the quality of the Compressed pulse in combination with the radial pulse that determines the patient's precise tissue aggregation condition.

Small Compressed Pulses (figure 118):

The small Compressed pulses are palpable as tiny masses with a defined peak. The relative hardness of these pulses determines the severity and chronic nature of the particular obstruction. Small compressed pulses of hard quality represent the most severe degree of tissue aggregation and potential malignancy.

Below is a description of the potential diagnostic correlations of the short compressed pulse located in each pulse position. If this pulse quality is palpable, it is recommended to have the patient seek diagnostic analysis from a medical doctor.

Right Yangwei: Pulmonary Embolism, COPD, Chronic Bronchitis, Asthma, Scar Tissue from Lung Surgery, Cystic Fibrosis, Wegener's Disease, Lung growths

Right Cun: Nasal Polyps, Intestinal Polyps, Hemorrhoids, Diverticulosis, Scar Tissue from Sinus Surgery, Deviated Septum

Right Guan: Stomach Ulcer, Stomach Polyps, Abdominal Aortic Aneurysm, Scar Tissue from Regional Surgery

Right Chi: Kidney Stones in the Right Ureter, Frozen Shoulder, Thoracic Osteophytes, Scar Tissue from Shoulder Surgery

Right Proximal: Cervical Osteophytes, Scar Tissue in the Thoracic and Cervical Regions from Surgery

Left Cun: Thoracic Aortic Aneurysm, Thoracic Trauma, Scar Tissue from Cardiac Surgery

Left Guan: Gallstones, Liver Cyst, Scar Tissue from Regional Surgery

Left Chi: Kidney Stones in the Left Ureter, Inguinal Hernia, Soft-Tissue Damage to the Knee (central Chi) / Hip (distal Chi) / Ankle (proximal Chi)

Left Chi In Women: Uterine Cyst, Uterine Fibroids, Scar tissue from Reproductive System Surgery

Left Chi in Men: Vasectomy Scar, Varicocele

Left Proximal: Scar Tissue in the Lumbar Region

Left Proximal In Women: Multiple Uterine Cysts, Uterine Fibroids, Polycystic Ovarian Disease, Scar Tissue from Reproductive System Surgery

Treatment Strategy: Strongly Invigorate the Blood / Break Up Blood Stasis

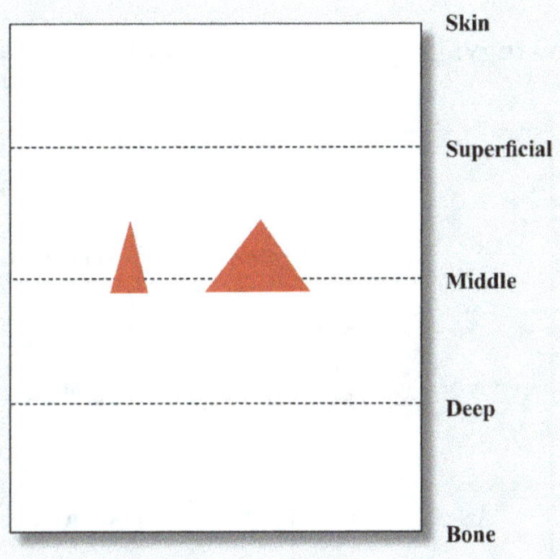

Figure 118: Small (soft or hard) Compressed pulses

Medium / Large Compressed Pulses (figure 119 & 120)

The medium and large Compressed pulses are palpable as convex masses that do not occupy the entire pulse position. These pulses are commonly found in the right and left Chi positions and represent inflammatory pain conditions of the corresponding anatomical regions. The larger Compressed pulses that occur with the Excess Heat (inflammation) pulse in the Chi positions, represent active inflammation and pain. The harder compressed pulses that occur without the Excess Heat (inflammation) pulse represent a more chronic condition of tissue damage with restricted circulation. In male patients, the bilateral presentation of medium or large Compressed pulses in both Chi positions can represent prostate issues, such as Benign Prostate Hyperplasia, Prostatitis, and Prostate disease.

Below is a description of the potential diagnostic correlations of the medium/large Compressed pulse located in the Chi positions.

Right Chi: Shoulder Complex Inflammation, Thoracic Region Inflammation

Left Chi: Knee (center Chi)/ Hip (distal Chi)/ Ankle (proximal Chi)

Treatment Strategy: Invigorate the Blood / Reduce Swelling

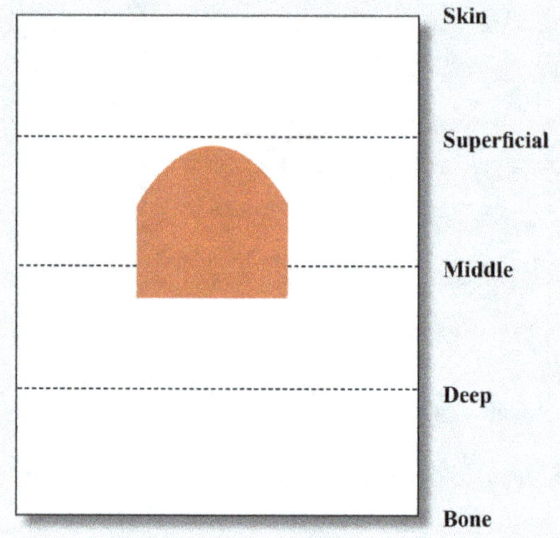

Figure 119: Medium (soft or hard) Compressed pulse

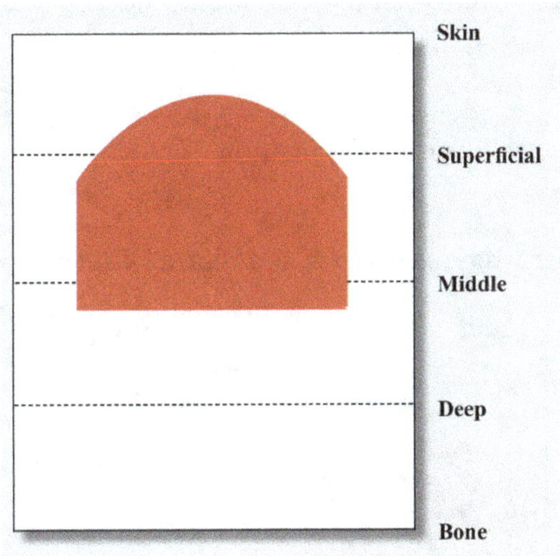

Figure 120: Large (soft or hard) Compressed pulse

Large-Extended Compressed Pulse (figure 121)

The large Compressed pulses that extend from the Chi to the Proximal positions represent inflammatory pain conditions of an expansive myofascial tissue region. When this pulse is palpable with an Excess Heat (inflammation) pulse, the large-extended Compressed pulse becomes elevated and forceful. In these cases, the corresponding tissue regions are in a state of active inflammation and pain. The presence of a large-extended Compressed pulse, without the Excess Heat pulse, represents a chronic pain condition with low-level inflammation and stagnant blood circulation.

Below is a description of the potential diagnostic correlations of the large-extended Compressed pulse located in the Chi and Proximal positions.

Right Chi: Cervical Region Inflammation, Thoracic Region Inflammation

Left Chi: Lumbar Region Inflammation

Treatment Strategy: Invigorate the Blood / Clear Heat

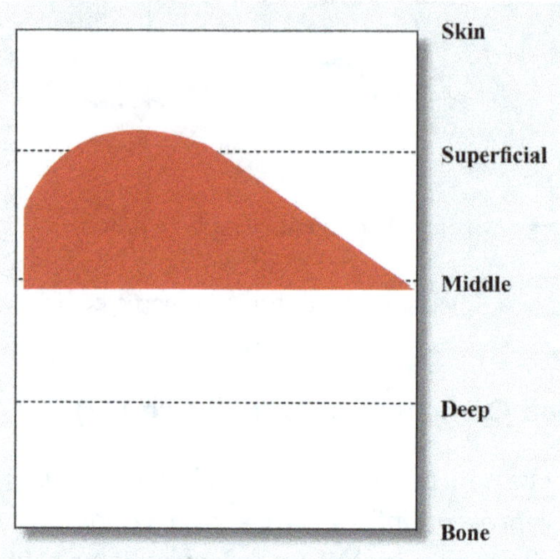

Figure 121: Large-Extended Compressed pulse

Systemic Pulses

The pulses described in this section represent pathologies that affect the entire radial pulse presentation. Each of these pathologies relates to a specific dysfunction of the heart or systemic cardiovascular dysfunction that can have a widespread impact on multiple health systems.

Up-Down pulse (figure 122)

In palpating the standard pulse, only the ascending aspect of the pulse wave is felt and provides diagnostic information. Contrarily, in palpating the Up-Down pulse, both the ascending and descending aspects of the pulse wave are felt. The western medical term for this pulse is the water-hammer pulse. The diagnostic fingers sharply elevate during the ascending phase of the pulse wave and then collapse in the descending phase. This creates a mechanical up-down sensation along the radial artery. This quality can result from an aortic valve regurgitation, generally due to aortic valve insufficiency and aortic stenosis. This pulse is most common in patients of senior age. With this patient group, do not mistake the Up-Down pulse as an Excess Heat (inflammation) pulse.

Treatment Strategy: Strongly Invigorate the Blood to Resolve Valvular Calcification

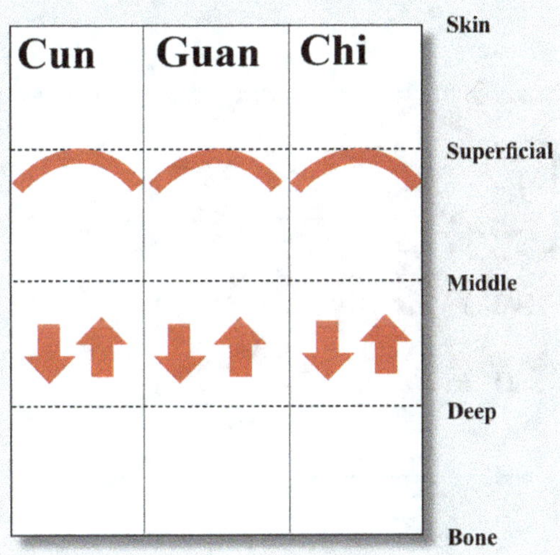

Figure 122: Up-Down pulse

Viscous Blood Pulse (figure 123)

The healthy pulses maintain a fluid water-like quality as a result of healthy blood composition. The blood circulating in the vessels contains plasma, red blood cells, white blood cells, and platelets. Plasma is mostly made up of water and includes proteins, clotting factors, electrolytes, nutrients and waste products.

The Viscous Blood pulse indicates a higher density of particles in the bloodstream. This issue can result from high blood lipids and glucose from poor diet, accumulated toxins/waste products, and blood disorders involving abnormal blood cell production.

In this case, the vessel boundaries are clearly palpable, but the fluid within the artery feels thick, viscous and sluggish.

Treatment Strategy: Invigorate the Blood / Detoxify the Blood

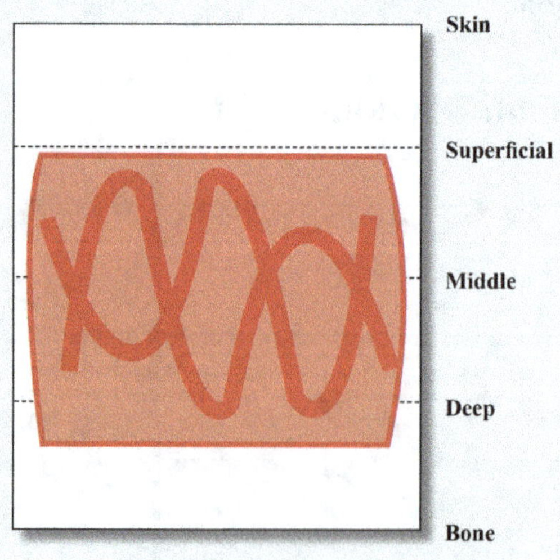

Figure 123: Viscous Blood pulse

Stiff Pulse (figure 124)

The optimal circulation of blood and nutritive factors throughout the body requires elastic and flexible arteries, especially near the heart. With age and compounded health issues such as elevated cholesterol, high blood pressure, diabetes and obesity the arterial walls can stiffen, due to calcification, and lose the ability to expand as blood circulates throughout the body. This can lead to restricted blood circulation to the body's organ and tissue systems. In western medicine, the term for this condition is arteriosclerosis. This condition can lead to coronary artery disease, peripheral artery disease, carotid artery disease, aneurysms and chronic kidney disease.

The Stiff pulse represents the hardening of the arterial vessel system. With this pulse, the entire radial artery is palpable as a hard, slightly thick, wiry pulse that is resistant to pressure. This compromised vessel structure limits optimal blood circulation to both internal and external regions of the body and may provoke a myriad of health conditions.

Treatment Strategy: Strongly Invigorate the Blood, Vasodilate and Soften Vessel Walls

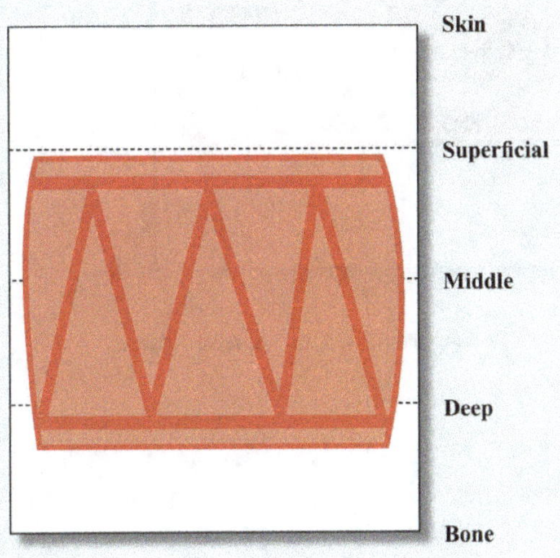

Figure 124: Stiff pulse

Thick-Swollen Pulse (Figure 125)

Atherosclerosis is the narrowing of the inside diameter of the arterial vessel wall by a combination of accumulated lipids, proteins, cholesterol, calcium and the proliferation of vessel cells. This swollen condition may partially or entirely obstruct blood circulation along the arterial distributions to the heart, brain, pelvis, legs, arms or kidneys. This condition can also lead to coronary artery disease, peripheral artery disease, carotid artery disease, aneurysms and chronic kidney disease.

The Thick-Swollen pulse represents a systemic narrowing of the inside diameter of the arterial walls due to inflammation and cell proliferation. With this pulse, the entire radial artery wall feels slightly thick and swollen. Increased palpatory pressure also demonstrates a spongy quality of the vessel wall.

Treatment Strategy: Invigorate the Blood / Reduce Swelling

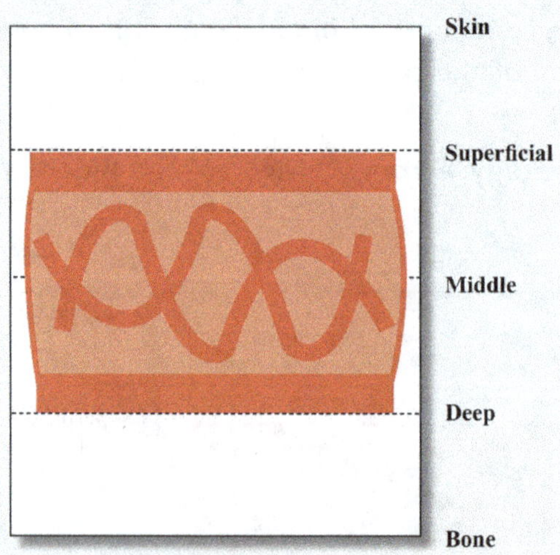

Figure 125: Thick-Swollen pulse

Pulse Rate

In MPD, the detailed findings of the radial pulse are the most definitive diagnostic tool. The pulse rate is a secondary measure that contributes to the patient's diagnosis. Note that certain health conditions and usage of specific medications may alter the pulse rate.

The average pulse rate is approximately 72 beats per minute (bpm).

Any pulse rate between 70-80 bpm is within reasonable limits. Note that the standard pulse rate of an endurance athlete may be lower than these limits.

The pulse rate of 80 bpm or higher is too fast and often indicates an Excess condition, Heat (inflammation) condition or a combination of both. It is important to note that a functional deficiency in the heart can also cause an elevated heart rate. The presence of an infection or abscess can generate a pulse rate of 120 bpm or higher with a concurrent fever.

The pulse rate of 60 bpm or lower (in a non-athlete) is too slow and often indicates a Deficiency condition, Cold condition or a combination of both. The use of beta-blockers, calcium channel blockers, and digitalis glycosides (Digoxin) often lower the patient's heart rate.

Conclusion

This text is designed to provide every health practitioner with the fundamental steps to thoroughly understand and effectively apply MPD in the clinical setting. MPD has been the primary diagnostic tool of the Acupuncture and Wellness Center, P.S. for the last twenty years in the treatment of over 500,000 patient visits. Unique to the clinic is the implementation of four to five month herbal treatment plans, which allow for the continuous analysis and treatment of the patient's condition to maximal resolution. Based on the constant care of thousands of patients, the MPD methods are in a perpetual state of refinement to maximize the effectiveness of Chinese herbal therapies. An ever expanding group of practitioners now employ MPD as a primary tool in clinics all over the world. The relationships forged with the thousands of practitioners at MPD live seminars, on our educational platform - Doane.us, and with those that train in-person at the clinic provide continual insights that make MPD progressively more efficient and effective in the clinical setting.

In my thirty years of studying Chinese Medicine, I am continually amazed that a 2500-year-old indigenous medicine from China can have such a positive dramatic effect on our overall health. Western medicine's failure to treat chronic diseases has been an open door for Chinese Medicine to rise to prominence in the treatment of long-standing health conditions. The only ancient diagnostic technique left to learn to increase the effectiveness of Chinese medicine today is the ability to analyze pulses correctly. MPD (Medical Pulse Diagnosis) will dramatically improve the skill of all Chinese Medicine practitioners worldwide. It is my honor to present this wonderful method to you in its most comprehensive form yet.

Appendix 1

Pulse Positions - Anatomical Correspondences and Conditions

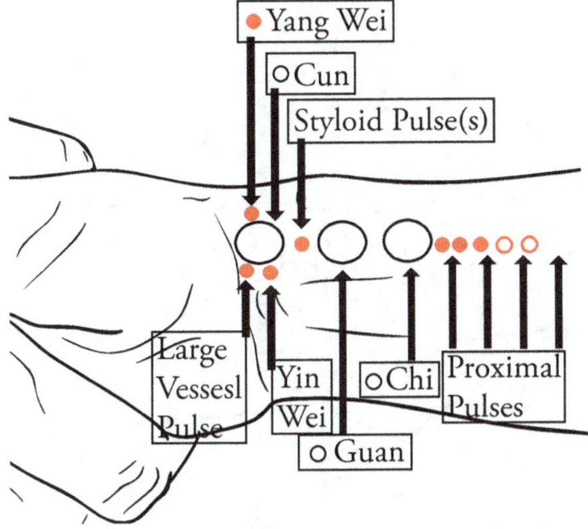

Locations of Cun, Guan, Chi, Yang Wei, Yin Wei,
Large Vessel, Styloid and Proximal Pulses

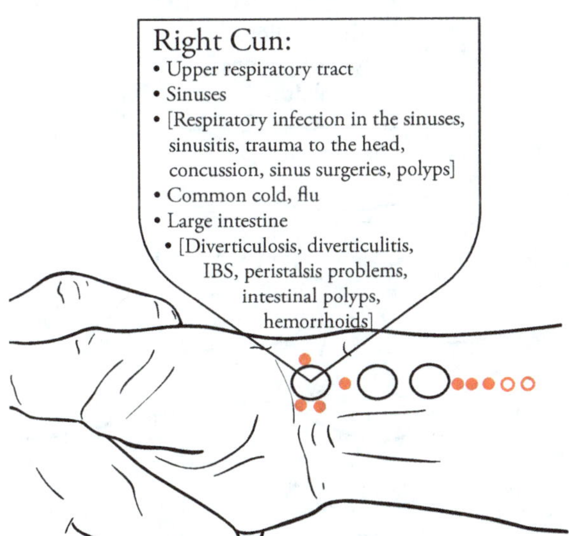

Right Cun pulse position and its correspondence to the
upper respiratory tract, the large intestine, and associated conditions.

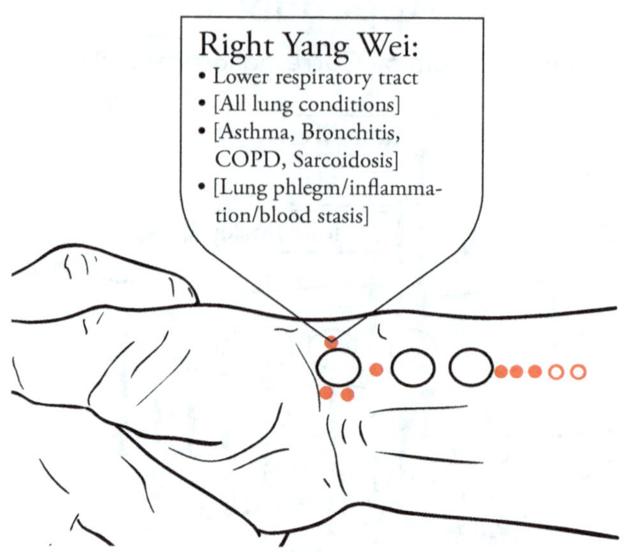

Right Yang Wei pulse position and its correspondence to the lower respiratory tract and associated conditions

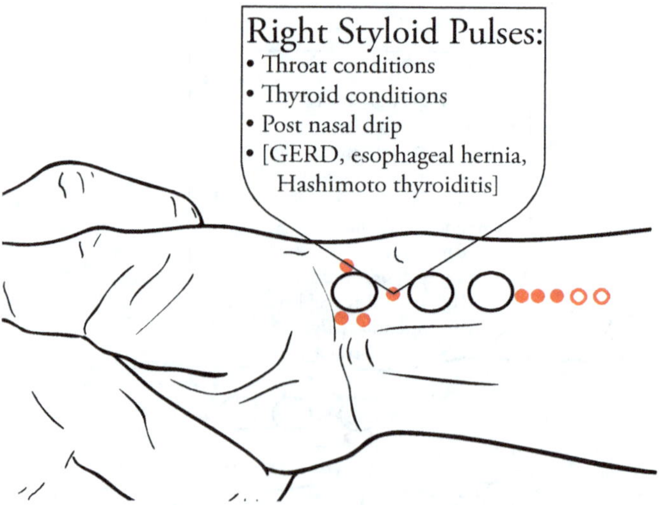

Right Styloid pulses and its correspondence to throat diseases, e.g., thyroid gland diseases, post-nasal drip, esophageal hernia and gastric reflux

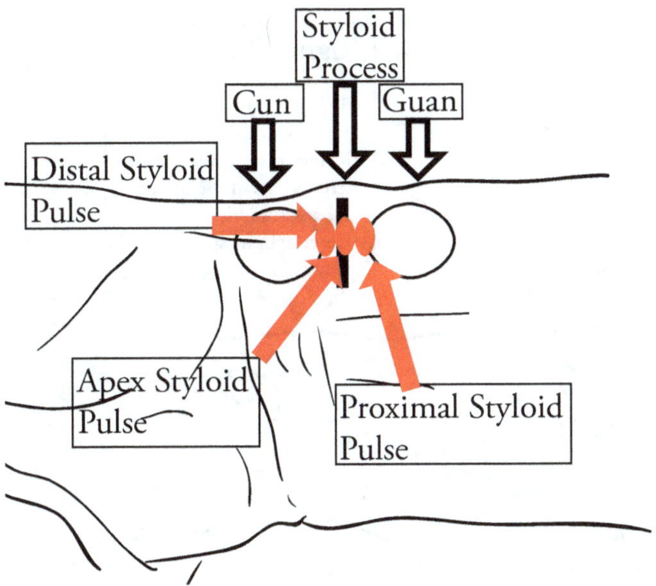

Location of the Distal, Apex and Proximal Styloid pulse positions

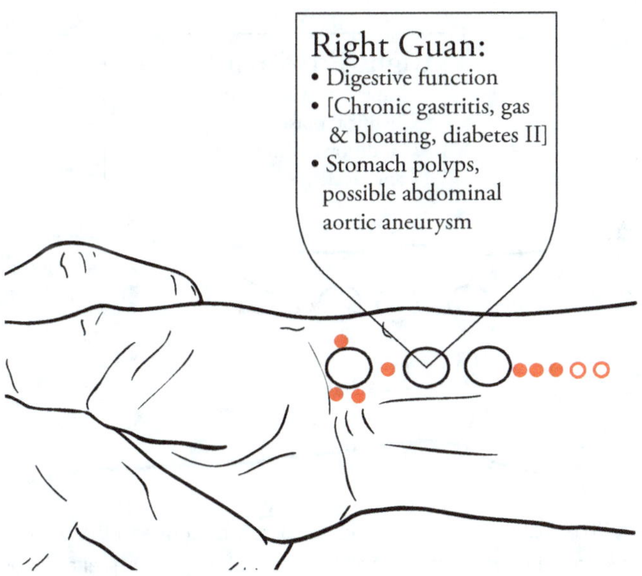

Right Guan pulse position and its correspondence to
gastrointestinal conditions related to the stomach and pancreas

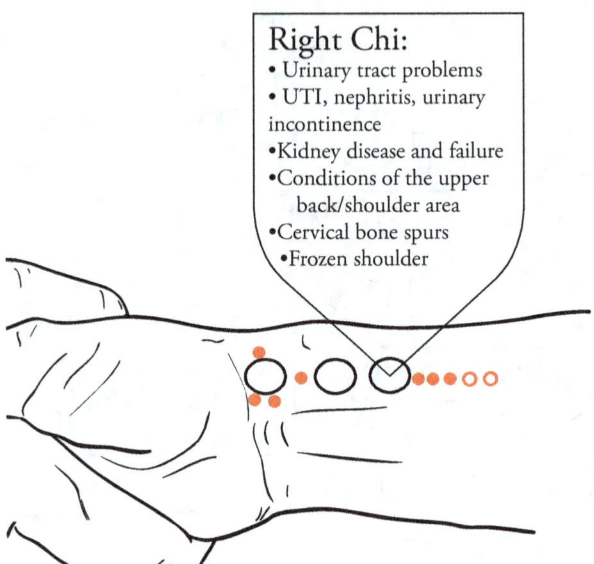

Right Chi pulse position and its correspondence to the kidneys, urinary system, thoracic and shoulder regions.

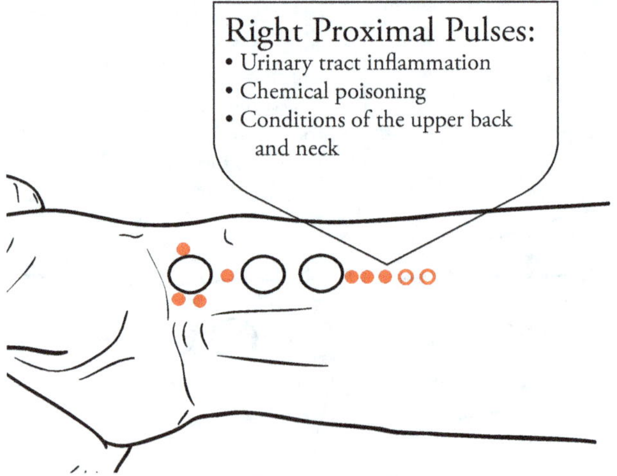

Right Proximal pulse position and its correspondence to the upper thoracic/cervical region, urinary system, and potential chemical poisoning

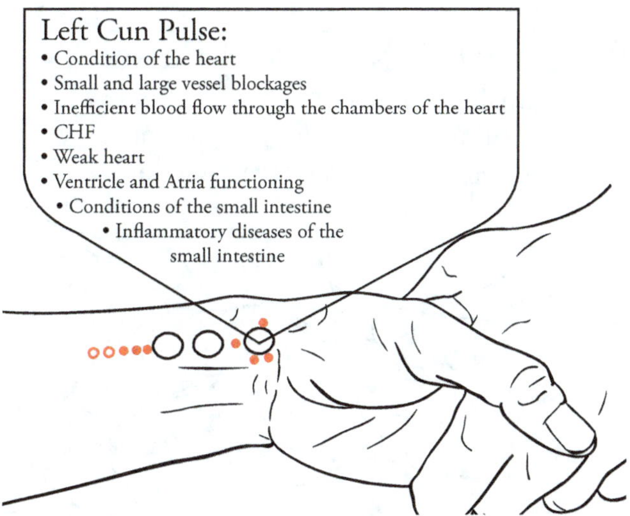

Left Cun pulse position and its correspondence to the condition of the heart, pericardium and small intestine

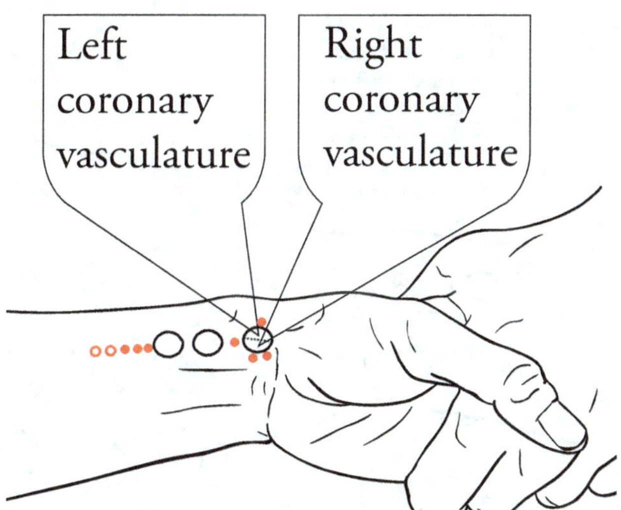

Left Cun pulse position and the location of the left and the right side coronary vasculature

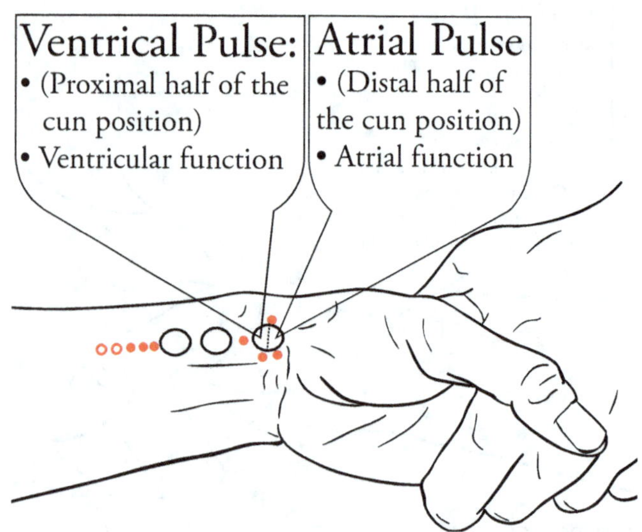

Left Cun pulse position and location of the atrial and ventricular regions

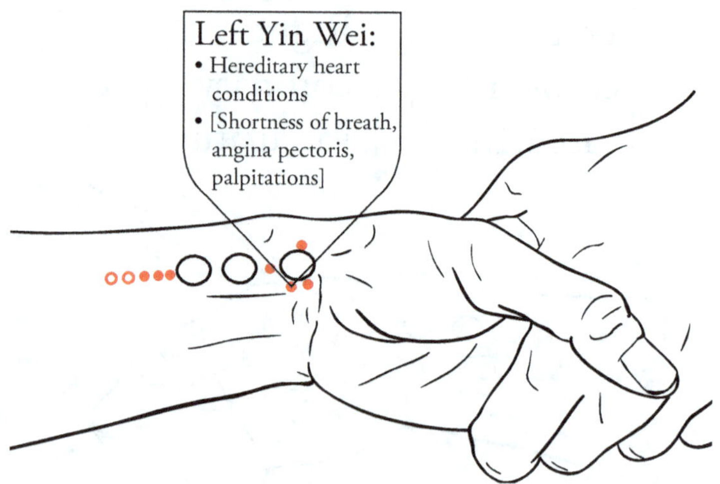

Left Yin Wei Pulse and its correspondence to
hereditary heart conditions and heart symptoms

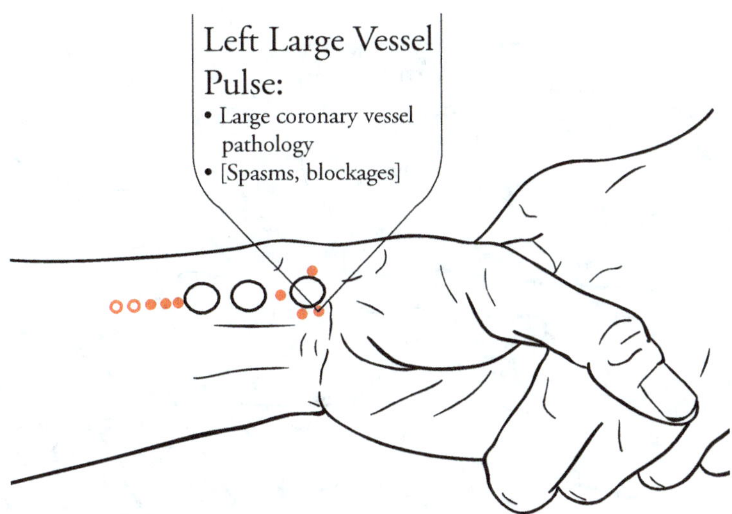

Left Large Vessel Pulse and its correspondence to
large coronary vessel pathology

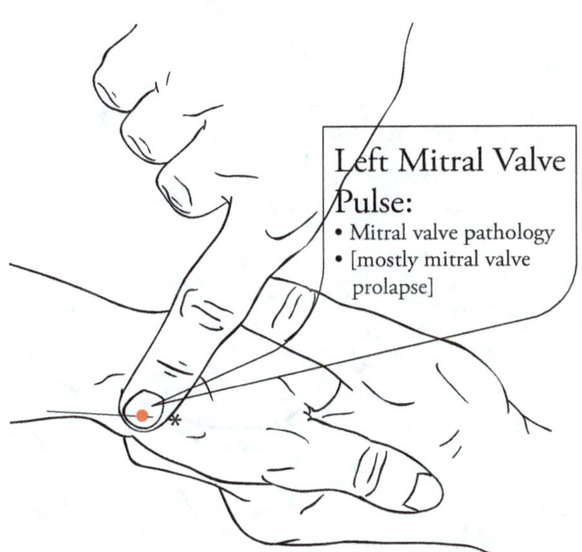

Left Mitral Valve Pulse and its correspondence to
heart valve conditions (most commonly mitral valve dysfunction)

(*Abductor pollicis longus tendon)

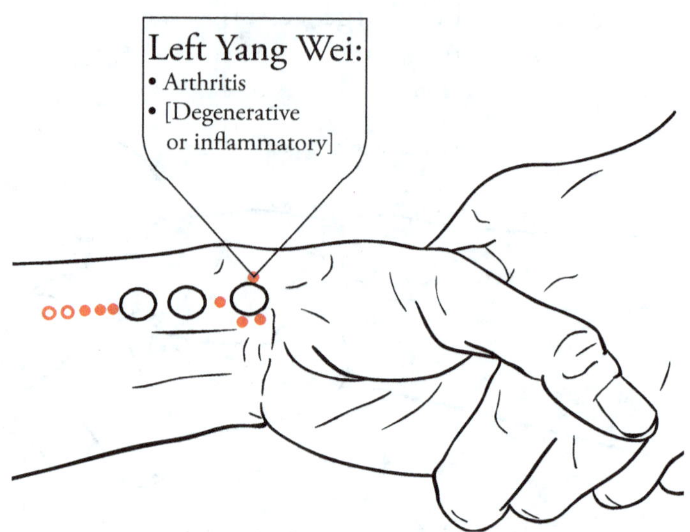

Left Yang Wei pulse postion and its correspondence to
arthritis and other rheumatoid disorders

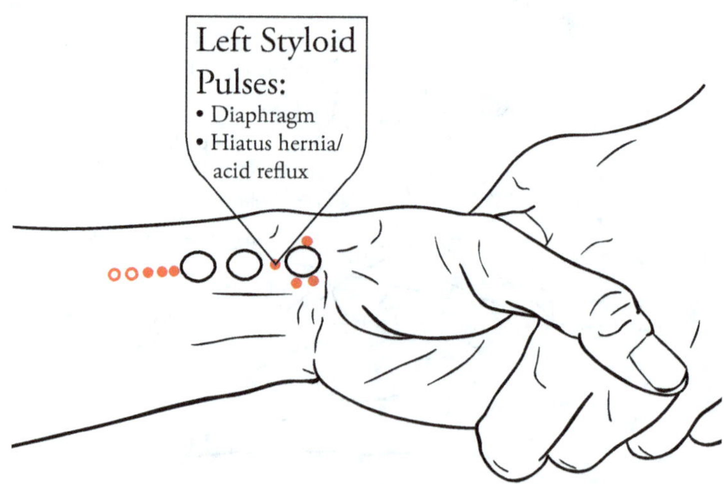

Left Styloid pulse postion and its correspondence to the
diaphragm, gastric reflux, hiatal hernia

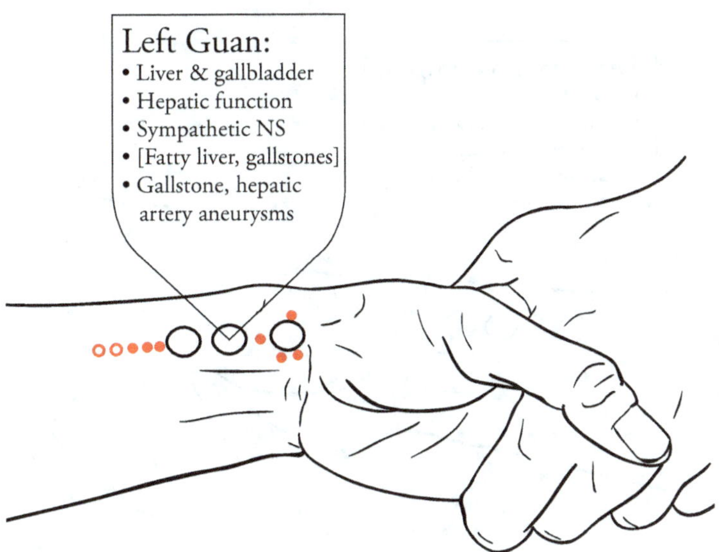

Left Guan pulse position and its correspondence to liver
and gallbladder conditions and mental/emotional conditions

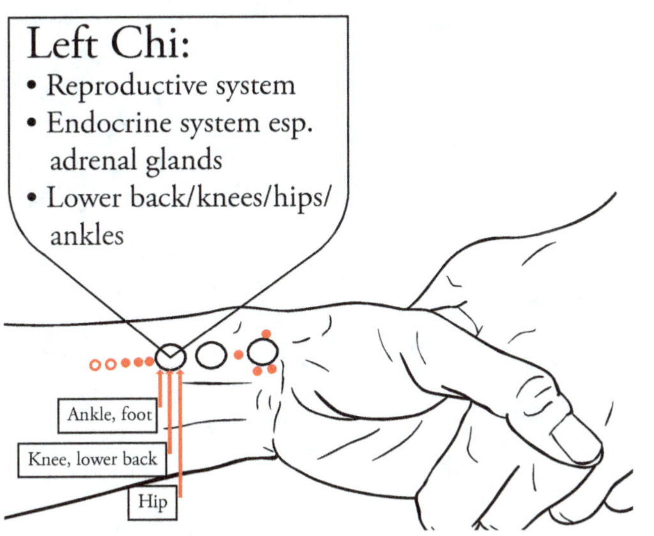

Left Chi pulse position and its correspondence to the reproductive system,
endocrine system (e.g., adrenal glands), knee, hip and ankle regions

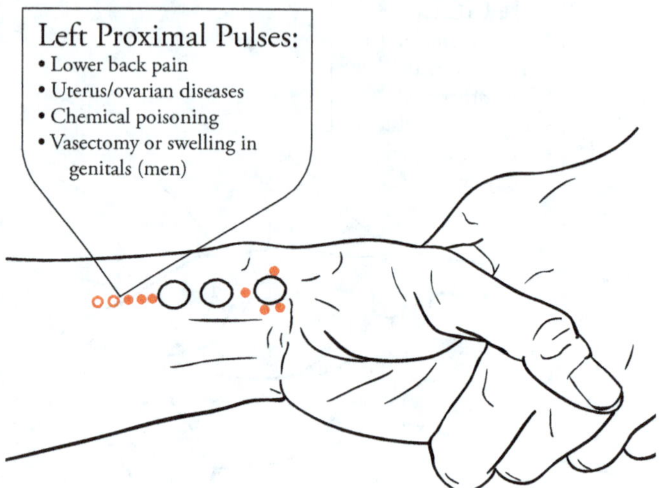

Left Proximal pulse position its correspondence to conditions of the lumbar region, uterus/ovarian conditions, chemical poisoning, vasectomy or prostate enlargement

Appendix 2

Variability in Pulse Analysis

Certain variations in the pulse are possible in response to the use of pharmaceuticals, recreational drugs, emotional states, patient build and other factors.

Pharmaceuticals

It is well known that many pharmaceuticals can alter the function or damage internal organ systems. Therefore, there are definite pulse variations due to the use of pharmaceuticals. Clinically, the only consistent and misleading variation is with patients using Beta Adrenergic Blockers (Beta Blockers). This medication will artificially slow the pulse and may lead to the false interpretation of Deficiency or Cold conditions. Check for patient usage of this pharmaceutical class, when the patient's overall signs/symptoms do not match the slow pulse quality.

The following is a list of common Beta Adrenergic Blocking Agents (Beta Blockers):

- acebutolol hydrochloride (Sectral)

- atenolol (Tenormin)

- betaxolol hydrochloride (Kerlone)

- bisoprolol fumarate (Zebeta)

- carteolol hydrochloride (Cartrol)

- carvedilol (Coreg)

- esmolol hydrochloride (Brevibloc)

- metoprolol (Lopressor, Toprol XL)

- penbutolol sulfate (Levatol)

- nadolol (Corgard)

- nebivolol (Bystolic)

- pindolol (Visken)

- propranolol (Inderal, InnoPran)

- timolol maleate (Blocadren)

- sotalol hydrochloride (Betapace)

References

Anzaldua, D. (2010). An Acupuncturist's Guide to Medical Red Flags & Referrals. Boulder, CO: Blue Poppy Press.

Beers, M. H. (2006). The Merck Manual. (T. V. Jones & R. S. Porter, Eds.) (18th ed.). Kenilworth, NJ: Merck.

Benjamin, E. J., Blaha, M. J., Chiuve, S. E., Cushman, M., Das, S. R., Deo, R., … Muntner, P. (2017). Heart Disease and Stroke Statistics 2017 Update: A Report from the American Heart Association. Circulation (Vol. 135).

Center for Disease Control: Heart Disease and Stroke Cost America Nearly $1 Billion a Day in Medical Costs, Lost Productivity. (n.d.). Retrieved March 12, 2017, from http://www.cdcfoundation.org/%0Apr/20   15/heart-disease-and-stroke-cost-america-nearly-1-billion-daymedical-%0Acosts-lost-productivity

Chang, J. (1995). Pulsynergy: A Pulse Diagnosis Manual. (n.p.): Author.

Cleveland Clinic Team. (n.d.). 22 Amazing Facts About Your Heart. Retrieved August 2, 2016, from https://health.clevelandclinic.org/2016/08/22-amazing-facts-about-your-heart-infographic

Dharmananda, S. (n.d.). The Significance of Pulse Diagnosis in the Modern Practice of Chinese Medicine. Retrieved March 12, 2017, from http://www.itmonline.org/arts/pulse.htm

Flaws, B. (2006). The Classic of Difficulties: A Translation of the Nan jing. Boulder, CO: Blue Poppy Press.

Hsu, E. (2010). Pulse Diagnosis in Early Chinese Medicine: The Telling Touch. Cambridge: Cambridge University Press.

Lowe, G. D. O., Lee, A. J., Rumley, A., Price, J. F., & Fowkes, F. G. R. (1997). Blood Viscosity and Risk of Cardiovascular Events: The Edinburgh Artery Study. British Journal of Haematology, 96(1), 168–173. https://doi.org/10.1046/j.1365-2141.1997.8532481.x

Mozaffarian, D., Benjamin, E. J., Go, A. S., Arnett, D. K., Blaha, M. J., Cushman, M., … Turner, M. B. (2015). Heart Disease and Stroke Statistics-2015 Update : A Report from the American Heart Association. Circulation (Vol. 131).

Nayor, M., Enserro, D. M., Vasan, R. S., & Xanthakis, V. (2016). Cardiovascular Health Status and Incidence of Heart Failure in the Framingham Offspring Study. Circulation Heart Failure, 9(1), 29–322.

Neeb, G. R. (2006). Blood Stasis: China's Classical Concept in Modern Medicine. London: Churchill Livingstone;

Saladin, K. (2004). Anatomy & Physiology: The Unity of Form and Function (3rd ed.). New York, NY: McGraw-Hill Education.

Shen-Qing, L., & Morris, W. (2011). Li Shi-Zhen's Pulse Studies: An Illustrated Guide. Bejing: People's Medical Publishing House.

Shu-He Wang, & Shou-Zhong, Y. (1997). The Pulse Classic: A Translation of the Mai jing. Boulder, CO: Blue Poppy Press.

Unschuld, P. U. (2016). Nan Jing: The Classic of Difficult Issues (2nd ed.). (n.p.): University of California Press.

Walsh, S., & King, E. (2007). Pulse Diagnosis: A Clinical Guide. London: Churchill Livingstone.